THE LAST LABOUR OF THE HEART

The Last Labour of The Heart

A Novel
By Paul Vasey

Black Moss
2005

National Library of Canada Cataloguing in Publication

Vasey, Paul
    The last labour of love / Paul Vasey.

ISBN 0-88753-407-4

    I. Title.

PS8593.A78L38 2005   C813'.54   C2005-901888-7

Designed by Karen Veryle Monck

Published by Black Moss Press at 2450 Byng Road, Windsor, Ontario
N8W 3E8. Black Moss books are distributed in Canada and the U.S.
by Firefly Books, Firefly Books Ltd., 66 Leek Crescent, Richmond
Hill, ON Canada L4B 1H1. All orders should be directed there.

Black Moss would like to acknowledge the generous support to its
publishing program from the Canada Council and the Ontario Arts
Council for their publishing programs.

ONTARIO ARTS COUNCIL
CONSEIL DES ARTS DE L'ONTARIO

Le Conseil des Arts | The Canada Council
du Canada | for the Arts

For Laura

• • •

Thanks to my family–
Marilyn, Kirsten, Mark, Gemma and Adam—
and to my friend Mary Ann Mulhern
for their careful reading of the manuscript
and their suggestions for strengthening it.

Many thanks to Wendell Berry for permission to use a portion of his poem "Awake At Night" as the epigraph for this novel, and a line from that poem as its title. The poem is to be found in *Wendell Berry's Collected Poems 1957-1982*, published by North Point Press; Farrar Strauss and Giroux, New York (1984).

The lines by Henry Wadsworth Longfellow found on page 32 are from the poem "God's Acre" found in *The Poetical Works of H.W. Longfellow* published by Collins Clear-Type Press, London & Glasgow.

The lines by Charles Bukowski found on page 48 and thereafter are from his collection *The Days Run Away Like Wild Horses Over The Hills,* Black Sparrow Press, Santa Barbara California (1979).

The line by William Wordsworth found on page 81 is from *The Selected Poetry and Prose of Wordsworth,* New American Library, New York (1980).

The lines by Bruce Cockburn found on page 93 are from the song "All The Diamonds in The World" from his 1974 album "Salt, Sun and Time", Columbia Records.

The lines by Rainer Maria Rilke found on page 94 and 106 are from *Duino Elegies,* translated by David Young, published by W.W. Norton & Company, New York (1992).

The lines by Thomas Merton found on page 95 are from his book *The Seven Storey Mountain,* published by Harcourt, Brace Jovanovich, New York (1948).

The lines by Bernard Malamud found on page 108 are from his novel *Dubin's Lives;* Farrar Strauss Giroux, New York (1979).

The lines by Rainer Maria Rilke found on page 112 are from *Letters To A Young Poet,* translated by Stephen Mitchell; Random House, New York (1984).

There is an allusion on page 125 to the poem "Once and For All" by Delmore Schwartz. The complete poem is to be found in *Selected Poems, Summer Knowledge;* New Directions (1967).

The lines by Algernon Charles Swinburne found on page 142 are from "Felise", published in *Selected Poems,* edited by L.M. Findlay, Carcanet Press, Manchester (1987).

But the end, too, is part
of the pattern, the last
labour of the heart:
to learn to lie still,
one with the earth
again, and let the world go.

Awake at Night
Wendell Berry

Aunt Lou had decided to die. The thought had got into her head and there was no getting it out. So said the nurse who called Benjamin Miles from the nursing home in Minneapolis. Lou had stopped eating. Wouldn't take a bite. She was shedding pounds the way a dog sheds fur. She can't weigh more than ninety pounds. She's skin, bones and sheer determination, said the nurse. She wants to die and she doesn't want anyone trying to stop her.

Had she tried to talk to Lou? Talk her out of it?

They'd talked till they were blue. There was no changing her mind. She was stubborn as stone.

All this came as news to Benjamin Miles.

It was his habit to call Lou every Sunday at suppertime. Every Sunday at suppertime Lou told him she was fine. Benjamin had no reason to disbelieve. Lou had seemed fine, had seemed happy. In fact, she'd seemed happier these past few weeks than she'd been in months. This had come as a relief to Benjamin, assuaging the guilt he felt whenever he thought of Lou and this traumatic year in her life.

Seven months earlier, February, still living in her south-side home – the home she'd shared with Bob for twenty-seven years, the home where she'd lived on alone the past nineteen – Lou had suffered a minor stroke. From the looks of it – nightie, no slippers, no housecoat – it appeared she'd been on her way in the middle of the night from bedroom to bathroom when the stroke felled her in the hallway between. A neighbour, alerted by closed window blinds and two Star Tribunes on the front stoop found Lou on the floor.

Lou spent a week in hospital before being transferred to the seniors' complex where she'd had the foresight a couple of years earlier to put herself on the waiting list. She stayed in the nursing-care wing of the home until April. Lou's doctor, her nurses, her friends and Benjamin all agreed it would be imprudent for her to return home. As luck would have it, a resident died two days later, freeing an apartment in the independent-living wing.

Perhaps a stroke of luck, Lou said – just the trace of a smile.

Lou hadn't been at the top of the apartment list but given her medical situation and the fact she would be paying with her own funds – no messy dealings with private medical insurers – Lou moved up the list and into the apartment the first week of May.

Benjamin took a week off work and he and Kathleen drove down from Canada to help Lou make the move.

We'll have to be ruthless, said Lou. They had been. Benjamin and Kathleen brought box after box to the living room where Lou sat in her favourite armchair and determined what would go to The Home and what would go to the dumpster in the driveway.

By week's end, Aunt Lou was sitting in her new apartment in her favourite armchair, surrounded by her favourite pieces of furniture – a walnut side table and brass lamp (Robert's gift on their third anniversary), the bureau from her bedroom set, her writing desk – and her most cherished photographs, phonographs and knick-knacks.

The day before Benjamin and Kathleen headed back to Canada, Benjamin took Lou to an appliance store – a little family-owned affair near her house where she'd been doing business for more than forty years – and bought her a new television and a new needle for her record-player. The owner remarked that he remembered selling Lou that very record-player and to prove this was not merely salesman's chatter, he yanked open a filing drawer, thumbed through some folders and in a matter of moments produced the carbon-copy of the original bill. RCA Victor, he said. Good for a lifetime.

With the television in a cardboard box in the back seat and the record-player needle in Lou's purse, they drove to Baker's Square which, though a new place and a franchise, was one of Lou's favourites. Lou ordered chicken pot pie and – the real reason for their coming – a piece of French silk pie, chocolate custard filling topped with whipped cream and chocolate shavings. Hardly a calorie in the entire thing, said Lou. And although she declared herself too full to finish the chicken pot pie she was able, after a few sips of tea, to work her way right through the French silk pie without any trouble at all. Benjamin took this for a very good omen.

A couple of hours later, when he bent down to kiss her goodbye, Lou put her stick-like arms around his neck and told him she was happy as a canary, told him she couldn't be happier or more comfortable, told him she felt blessed, told him he needn't worry his head about her. She'd be fine. Just fine.

Though her words were designed to comfort, Benjamin had not been comforted.

Like a politician, Lou had said all the right things but had not been able to muster the conviction to prop them up so that all her reassurances had the ring of a speech given once too often on the hustings.

Benjamin had been discomfited and tweaked with guilt almost halfway across the state of Wisconsin despite Kathleen saying, and repeating, that Lou would be fine. Just wait, you'll see. She'll actually be happy.

Hm.

Women's intuition: week by week, Lou seemed to get cheerier, had news to relate of the events in The Home – reading nights, sing-along nights, bingo nights, Sunday services. She seemed right in the swing of things. Lou had the janitor move her writing desk from the side wall, where Benjamin had positioned it, to the window wall so that sitting there she could look out and see the children playing in the fenced yard of the day-care center behind The Home. I didn't realize there was a day-care center back there. Neither did I, said Lou, until I heard the children the other morning. I thought it was birds, but it was the children talking and laughing. Better than birds.

And it was a joy to be able to watch the little ones playing on the swings and the slides, a joy to hear their voices, their laughter. It reminded her of the days when Anna and Aaron were just toddlers. Back in the early days. The voices of children elevate the spirit, said Lou. I am truly blessed. Benjamin had been a willing believer.

Even three weeks earlier, the last normal Sunday telephone conversation they'd had – Perry Como in the background scratchily singing Catch A Falling Star – Lou had seemed perfectly happy and content although she said, when quizzed, that lately she hadn't been taking part in any of the activities, save for Sunday services.

She enjoyed the Sunday services, especially Pastor Owen's sermons. He's got a lovely Jamaican accent, and he speaks loudly enough so that you can hear him, too. The sermons, and the hymns – How Lovely Is Thy Dwelling Place; Jesus, Thou Divine Companion; Alleluia, The Strife is O'er. Those and many more.

You want to hear something funny? Sure, he said. Some of the women take their teeth out when they sing. Their teeth? I guess if they really start singing their teeth can pop out, so they take them out as a precaution and set them on the pew. That is funny. That's not the funny part, she said. What's the funny part? The funny part is, sometimes they're in such a fervour they forget to put their teeth back in. They get up from their pews and they're still humming the hymns and they just wander out of the chapel and go back to their rooms and their apartments and there are false teeth here and there throughout the chapel, two or three sets, sometimes more. So at lunch time, the nurse comes in to the dining room with a tray, three or four sets of choppers on it, and she'll hold up the tray and sing out: Anyone lose anything lately? And you ought to see everyone – hands going to mouths all around the room. Lou laughed and Benjamin, eight hundred miles south and east, laughed along with her. He hung up the phone feeling very good.

I hate to say I told you so, said Kathleen, but I told you so.

Then things changed. Things changed in a hurry.

The Tuesday following the false-teeth call, Aunt Lou went down to the dining room for supper. Everything seemed fine. They served fish and chips and she ate every last French fry, then polished off a piece of apple pie and lingered over tea, chatting with her table-mates – even the one who dominated the conversation with stories of her daughters who had married well and were very comfortable, a woman of whom Lou was not especially fond but who might, she thought, have been sent to try her capacity for charity and test her level of tolerance. And I can tell you this: you'd need a tankful of charity and a reservoir of tolerance to put up with the likes of her.

Wednesday morning, Lou didn't come down for breakfast. When a nurse used a pass-key to open her door and check on her, Lou, sitting in her armchair, looked up from her book, said the last time she checked there was still a law against the invasion of privacy, said she didn't feel like breakfast, said she was going to stay in her apartment, said the door that let you in will let you out. When the nurse returned several minutes later with a breakfast tray and told Lou she had to eat something, Lou said the nurse might benefit from a hearing test, then pursed her lips, crossed her arms in front of her chest and gave the nurse a vigorous shake of the head. When the nurse brought lunch, the breakfast tray was untouched. When another nurse brought supper, the lunch tray was untouched. When the night nurse brought Lou's pills in a little paper cup, Lou slapped her hand away, sending the pills skittering under the bureau, under the bed. Lou ordered the nurse out of the apartment.

This went on for three days.

Lou began to lose weight though, at just more than one hundred pounds, she didn't have all that much to lose. She lost strength and became disoriented, didn't know what day it was, wasn't certain where she was. The nurses called the doctor. The doctor ordered her removed to the nursing-care wing at the far end of the complex. Lou was hooked up to a medication IV and a feeding tube, both of which she ripped out. She was hooked up again, and again she ripped out the tubes. She told the nurses and then the doctor that she wanted to die.

The doctor asked why.

That, said Lou, is a matter between The Almighty and Yours Truly.

She told the doctor and the nurses to leave her alone.

She told them that unless they did so she would call her attorney and her attorney – avaricious badger that he was – would sue them for all they were worth. Them, and the nursing home.

Can't you let a little old lady die in peace?

Lou turned her back on them, shut her eyes and pretended to sleep. Then she slept.

The doctor told the nursing supervisor to contact Lou's next of kin.

As for next of kin, Benjamin was it.

More or less.

Benjamin's father had been an accountant who specialized in bringing companies back from the brink. For this, he was handsomely rewarded. Sometimes, when the owners had given up the ghost, Benjamin's father would buy the company, resuscitate it, restore it to health and then sell it. For this, he was rewarded even more handsomely. Some companies he retained and nurtured and thus it was that Luther Miles wound up with a miniature empire of factories in six states and four provinces and thus it was that he had become a wealthy man.

Robert was a salesman. He worked for a furniture company which Benjamin's father had been called in to save. Robert was the only salesman – very healthy accounts – Benjamin's father hadn't fired. Over the next year, the two had become friendly. When Benjamin's father moved on – the company on firm footing and Robert in the general manager's chair – they kept in touch.

A couple of years later, Benjamin's father bought a bankrupt clothing company. The company had a good line but had been run – and run into the ground – by the drunken and incompetent grandson of its founder: a melancholy but not unfamiliar story.

Benjamin's father made Robert an offer he couldn't refuse: president and minority partner.

Thus it was that Robert had become wealthy in a minor way and forever indebted to this stranger who had swaggered into his life – cape, cane and bowler hat – and changed it in the most surprising way. And thus it was – more importantly – that Benjamin's extended family had been extended by two. Lou and Bob became his Godparents. This was back in the 40s, just after The War. Benjamin had no memory of Lou and Bob from those years; had only a few black and white snapshots of these smiling strangers smiling at the Kodak from a great distance in time and space.

Not long after taking their vows, Lou and Bob were forced by circumstance to fail to keep a close and watchful Christian eye on little Benjamin Miles.

Benjamin's father had followed the trail of insolvency and opportunity through Wisconsin, into Michigan and across the border into Ontario. The friendship between the couples faded like an old photograph.

Nevertheless, as far back as Benjamin could remember, he could remember receiving Easter cards and birthday cards, Thanksgiving cards (American and Canadian), Christmas cards and cards commemorating any other occasions and milestones – graduations, get well – Lou could think of. Plus, Lou was a killer note writer: wrote notes whenever the mood struck her, which was often. When he was old enough, Benjamin began to write back, became a kind of pint-sized pen-pal to a woman whose perfume he could sometimes detect on her stationery. Lou's cards and letters were filled with the news of the day, the news of her life. She would ask questions: what did you think of the Russians launching the satellite? Isn't that exciting? Do you think one day we'll send spaceships to the Moon, or to Mars?; or, a decade later: were you watching the Moon landing? Your Uncle Bob and I went out into the back yard last night with our binoculars and looked up at the Moon. Wasn't it strange to think that someone was actually up there, walking around? Did you go out and look at the Moon too? I fancied you did. It was fun to think that you were standing where you were and I was standing where I was, miles and miles apart, and that we were doing the same thing at the same time. It was almost as though you and I were standing side by side and talking about it. Do you think thoughts like that as well?

Serious questions. And she'd expect serious replies in the return mail.

She wanted to know what he thought of events in the news – racial strife in Alabama; the development of something called a computer (do you think one day we'll have such things in our homes, the way we now have typewriters?); the awful scourge of polio (I hope you're taking every precaution: staying out of crowds and not using public drinking fountains); the assassination of President Kennedy and, five years later, the assassination of his brother and, that same year, the killing of Martin Luther King. (Isn't it horrible and frightening that hatred can burn so hot in the hearts of some people as to make them pick up a gun and kill another human being? It is the ultimate failure of civilization, don't you think?) Now and then – always for birthdays and Christmas, but sometimes for no apparent reason at all – Lou would send packages containing gifts the likes of which Benjamin had never seen: a wood carving of an owl, a tortoise-shell fountain pen, a silk scarf, a bone-handled pocket knife, aviator sunglasses, an illustrated book about the history of the automobile.

Who is this Lou? Kathleen wondered when, after their wedding, she too began receiving cards and letters and surprising gifts.

Why don't we go visit them? Kathleen wondered a couple of years later, after they'd called Lou and Bob to announce Anna's birth.

We'd love it, Lou said over the phone, though Kathleen wasn't certain Lou's heart was entirely in the offer.

If it's a disaster, we can always make our excuses and leave after a day or two.

But that first visit had been far from a disaster, had in some strange way seemed like a kind of homecoming.

I feel as if I've known her all my life, said Kathleen.

The following summer, Benjamin and Kathleen made the trip again, this time with baby Aaron strapped in a car-seat beside Anna. Three and a half weeks after they'd hugged Lou and Bob, thanked them for the week's visit, promised to drive safely, promised to call as soon as they got home, Lou called with the news.

Bob had got up in the middle of the night with a case of heartburn, said he was going to get an Alka Seltzer and watch television for a little bit, told Lou not to worry, told Lou to go back to sleep.

When she woke in the morning, she found him in his recliner, the remote control in his lap, lifeless eyes fixed on an old John Wayne movie, Lou couldn't remember which one. One of the westerns – Somewhere In Sonora, Sagebrush Trail, one of those. Bob's favourites.

Kathleen and Benjamin, Anna and Aaron had come back west for the memorial service. When it was over – and many times in the ensuing years – Lou hugged Benjamin and said: it was meant to be that you would come back into my life. Just when I would need you the most. Sentimental, to be sure. But hard to argue otherwise.

As for kin of the bona-fide kind, Lou didn't have a relative on the planet. Mother and Father, brothers and sister had all gone to the grave many years since. So only Benjamin's name, Benjamin's and Kathleen's, appeared under 'next of kin' on the nursing home forms.

And so it was that, at least once a day, sometimes two or three times a day for the past couple of weeks, Benjamin had been on the phone with one nurse or another, had gotten to know them all by name and voice. As soon as they heard that odd northern accent, they'd address him by name, ask him how he was doing. They'd become pals.

Every day he hoped to hear from Linda or Deb, Denise or Sandra or Julie – the head nurse – that Lou had had a change of heart, was starting to eat, was getting stronger, would soon be able to return to her little apartment, to the rhythms of her life.

They were sorry to disappoint.

Each evening, a nurse would put the cordless phone to Lou's ear. Benjamin would ask Lou if she wanted to get well, wanted to get back to her apartment, her records, her books, her favourite things. Lou told him she did. He told her if she wanted to get well and get back to her apartment she would have to start eating, gain strength.

He felt like a schoolmaster, lecturing a recalcitrant child.

Lou promised. She said she would start eating. Said she would start with tomorrow's breakfast. Cross my heart.

She was lying.

She was giving him the brush-off, saying what she knew he wanted to hear just to get him off the phone. She wasn't eating a bite, wasn't taking her medications. She was losing weight and strength.

She's running on fumes, said Julie, the head nurse.

She's Scottish, said Benjamin.

Tell me about it, said Julie. So's my grandmother. And they're both stubborn as a tea stain.

Things couldn't go on like this, said Julie. If Lou didn't start eating, didn't start taking her medications, things would go from bad to worse in a hurry.

Benjamin asked what she meant by 'worse'.

She'll lapse into a coma and die.

Benjamin asked what she meant by 'in a hurry'.

A week, said Julie. Two at the most.

Benjamin told Julie he had a couple of options: he could catch a red-eye out of Detroit and be there first thing the next morning, or he could catch a flight Friday night and be there first thing Saturday morning.

I wouldn't wait until the weekend if I were you, said Julie.

So, just before midnight on the Monday night, Benjamin boarded a Sun Country charter – his travel agent having snagged a last-minute bargain – and a couple of hours later he was checking in at the Airport Holiday Inn in Minneapolis.

The irony of the names did not escape him.

Standing at the window of his hotel room, a Budweiser in hand, looking out at the skyline which he didn't quite recognize – didn't in fact know which direction was which – he stared at his own reflection. Not flattering. His curly hair was tousled, his shirt wrinkled, his stubbled face drawn.

He thought he might be facing north, in the general direction of St. Paul which led him to think of the zoo in St. Paul, the zoo he and Kathleen and Lou and the children had visited a few months earlier, a zoo whose name he could not recall.

Where was Kathleen when he needed her?

Hi.

How was the flight?

Fine. And the food was actually pretty good.

What'd you have?

A sandwich.

What kind?

Tuna. Or salmon.

There's a bit of a difference.

Well, whatever it was, it was fresh. I've got a question.

Kathleen waited eight hundred miles up the line for him to ask it.

Remember that zoo we visited last summer, with Lou and the kids?

Lake Como?

Thank you.

What's the question?

That was the question. I couldn't remember the name.

You woke me at two-thirty in the morning to ask me the name of a zoo?

Yah, said Benjamin, seems I did.

You could have looked it up in the yellow pages. Starts with Z.

I was just thinking about that lion.

Two-thirty in the morning and you're thinking about lions?

It's only one thirty here.

Benjamin?

18

Yes.

Say goodnight.

Goodnight.

Goodnight. There was a momentary silence, then Kathleen said 'Benjamin' and he said 'yes' and she said 'never mind' and he said 'what is it?' and she said 'nothing, I love you, get some sleep' and he said he loved her too and said goodnight again, as if for good measure, and hung up.

Lake Como had not been Benjamin's idea. He'd suggested a trip to the Minneapolis Zoo.

On their first visit to Minneapolis, twenty some years earlier, the five of them – Lou and Bob, Kathleen and little Anna and Benjamin – had driven out and spent the afternoon. The following year, the six of them – little Aaron in his stroller – had gone back. And the following year, the five of them – Bob recently dead, but still very much a presence everywhere they went – had returned, as they had returned each summer thereafter. A little ritual.

So, this past summer it seemed a matter of course. But Kathleen thought perhaps they should try another attraction, just for the sake of variety. Thumbing through the auto-club tourist guide, she'd spotted an advertisement for this other zoo, out in St. Paul. At Lake Como.

Oh, said Lou. Could we?

That sealed that.

The Lake Como zoo, as it turned out, was located beside the Lake Como Conservatory, an arboretum Lou would love to see one more time. The last time had been thirty-odd years before when she and Bob had packed a wicker basket – a basket that had made its final way from the basement to the dumpster – with iced tea and sandwiches and slices of Lou's famous apple pie and spent an idyllic afternoon on the lawn beside the lake beside the arboretum.

Do you think we might go there?

Here it is, said Kathleen, fingertip against some black letters on the Twin Cities map. It'll be a snap. We take this freeway to that freeway and there we are.

There weren't any freeways the last time we went, said Lou.

How long ago was this?

Just after the Ice Age. The one before the last one.

19

Benjamin belted Lou in the front passenger seat. Can you see over the dash?

No, said Lou. But I don't have to. I'm not driving. You are.

Kathleen sat on the edge of the back seat, her forearms on the back of the front seat, the road map dangling between Benjamin and Lou.

They suffered only brief patches of being lost.

Fifteen or twenty minutes later, Benjamin guided the car in to the parking lot beside the Conservatory – a cathedral of glass and white-painted metal circled by lawns which ended at a tree-sentinelled lake – the sight of which caused Lou to catch her breath and shudder and – oh my – reach for a Kleenex in her purse, whose clasp was giving her some difficulty.

Benjamin unfolded the wheelchair and for the next half hour they rolled Lou along the asphalt paths which circled the Conservatory and then went inside and nosed through the aisles bordered and overhung with exotic shrubs and plants and flowers whose names – orchids, azaleas, ranuculus, cyclamen, hydrangeas, snapdragons, freesias, ferns, palms – were thoughtfully displayed on little plaques stabbed into the earth at their bases. The place smelled like a jungle. There were green-houses extending to each side of the domed Conservatory – the dome being the Palm House – and it had taken them all of another hour stopping to sniff, stopping to look, stopping to touch, to make the rounds. Eventually they found their way to the sunken gardens – the one Lou remembered so vividly – at the center of which there was a reflecting pool in which carp finned about. At the end of the pond there was a statue of a young naked woman who seemed about to step from her pedestal and go for a walk among the carp.

At the far end of the reflecting pool, there was a bench, the very bench where all those years earlier Lou and Bob had sat after their picnic, sat and listened to the water streaming into the pond from the base of the statue, smelled the perfume of the orchids which, then as now, bloomed in profusion.

Kathleen was quick with the Kleenex. Lou dabbed her eyes, then blew her nose. Thank you.

I always keep them in my pocket, said Kathleen. In the event of emergencies.

I didn't mean about the Kleenex.

The three of them sat on the Lou-and-Bob bench and watched a couple of children kneeling at the edge of the pond, trying to catch a carp.

Lou told them about all the afternoons she and Robert used to steal away when he was on the road. Those were the days, just after their marriage, when they had moved from New York and Robert had taken his job as a salesman for Erklens Furniture. Lou used to go along on some of his trips, the longer ones – out west, down south. It was a little like taking holidays, just the two of them, with the company paying for the motels.

Robert loved the road trips, but hated being alone for hours on end. Natural-born salesman that he was, he had to have someone to talk with. Lou couldn't stand the thought of him being alone out there on the road. Lou wasn't jealous, though some of her friends assumed she was, assumed that was why she went along, to keep Robert under her thumb. That, she said, was never anything I had to concern myself with. Then, or ever. I just didn't want him out there in that featureless landscape with no one to talk to. I was terrified he'd fall asleep at the wheel and wind up in a ditch.

So, she went along as often as she could and on the long trips she did some of the driving. Lou used to love driving, especially back then and out there. The speed limit was how fast you felt like going. They had a '48 Mercury coupe, black as coal and a demon for speed. It had a flathead V-8 – one of the best engines Ford ever built – and all you had to do was touch the accelerator and you were flying.

I loved that car.

Eighty miles an hour, the windows open, she and Robert yelling to make themselves heard over the engine and the radio and the wind.

Mostly Robert yelling at me to slow down. Robert tended to be careful.

Lou loved the little towns and cities they visited: Cedar Rapids, Mason City, Davenport in Iowa; Falls City, Wahoo and West Point in Nebraska; Redfield, Watertown, Brookings in South Dakota; Albert Lea, Owatonna, Red Wing in Minnesota. Those and dozens of others.

Aren't they the prettiest names?

She never cared how long it took Bob to conclude his business with the furniture stores. Two hours, five hours, it was all the same to her.

She'd find a shaded bench in the town park and read . She remembers being in a classics phase back then. When she thought of those towns and those park benches, she thought of Conrad's Heart of Darkness, Hardy's Jude The Obscure, Charlotte Bronte's Jane Eyre, Jane Austen's Pride and Prejudice, Tolstoy's Anna Karenina, Dostoyevsky's Crime and Punishment.

She'd stroll around and look at shops and go in some place and have a soda – all those towns used to have a drug store with a soda fountain – and listen to the locals in their bibbed coveralls and base-ball caps and then back to the park and read, waiting for Bob to turn up. It had been a wonderful way to pass her days.

Certainly better than waiting at home.

And then there were the motels. Sly smile.

All in all, it was wonderful for her and it was wonderful for Robert.

He would have been lonely.

At the Lake Como zoo they had stopped to stare at the lemurs and the polar bear, the zebras and the timberwolf, the harbour seals and the penguins. But it was the lion which had startled and stopped them; a lion sitting atop an outcropping of cement which had been sculpted to look like a rock.

Benjamin had parked Lou's wheelchair so that the lion was direct-ly above her.

I never realized that lions had yellow eyes, said Kathleen.

The eyes seemed to be alive with a light of their own – a fierce and blazing light – and they stared at the lion for what seemed like a very long time – though probably not more than five minutes – and the lion stared right back.

I can't imagine what it must be like for him to live in there, said Lou. Can you?

It's no wonder they call him the King of the Jungle, said Kathleen.

What jungle? Lou asked Benjamin to wheel her away, wheel her outside. She felt like a breath of air and she'd love to go back and have another ride around The Conservatory.

Would they mind?

Did they have the time?

Benjamin and Kathleen said they wouldn't mind, they had all the time in the world.

22

I love zoos, said Lou. I've loved them ever since we visited the Bronx Zoo when I was a little girl living in New York. But they always make me sad.

Turn left out of the elevator. Navigate a corridor channel-markered with wheelchairs in which old ladies sat slumped and moaning, slumped and gape-jawed, slumped and stunned, slumped and asleep; a corridor which smelled of urine and bacon and feces and burnt toast and disinfectant.

Billy? Is that you Billy?

An arthritic claw snagged Benjamin's sleeve.

No. I'm sorry. I'm not Billy.

Why didn't you come earlier? Why did you wait all these years, Billy?

I'm not Billy.

There were tears in the old woman's eyes.

I thought you'd never come back, Billy. I thought I'd never see you again.

Benjamin patted her hand, then gently prised the fingers from his sleeve. It took some doing.

The nursing-care ward was large and rectangular; its predominant colour white, with maroon trimmings. The nursing station was in the center of the ward: an oasis of efficiency – computer screens and filing cabinets – demarked by a chest-high counter upon which a delivery someone had deposited a basket of fruit with a bouquet of Get Well balloons tethered by yellow ribbons to the wicker handle. One of the balloons was beginning to deflate. Benjamin poked the sagging balloon with a finger. One of the nurses looked up from the chart she'd been studying.

Can I help you?

Benjamin introduced himself.

You're the one from Canada?

The nurses smiled. One of them rose from her chair, extended her hand. I'm Julie. The head nurse. Nice to see you, in person. Your aunt is in 211. Over there. She indicated the direction with a nod of her head.

How's she doing?

Let's just say it's a good thing you decided to visit her now.

Julie consulted a careful row of clipboards and selected the one with 211 written in magic marker on a piece of masking tape on the metal clip. Julie studied the chart, then looked up at Benjamin.

She hasn't eaten in eight days. She's had water, but only occasionally. Now and then, she'll take her meds. But rarely. Julie shrugged and managed a half-hearted smile.

Maybe it'll make a difference that you've come. She's been anxious to see you.

There were fourteen patient rooms, two beds in each. There was a large window beside the door to each room so the nurses could keep an eye on the patients. Between the rooms and the nursing station there was a walkway about a dozen feet in width. Patients in wheelchairs were going in slow circles, not all in the same direction, not all in complete control of their vehicles. One woman had only the use of her right leg and right arm. She used her good foot and her good hand to propel her wheelchair in slow left-turning circles until she had nosed herself up against the wall.

Help me, she said. Someone please help me.

Benjamin pulled the wheelchair back from the wall, turned it around and aimed the woman in the direction of the far wall.

A semi-circle of wheelchairs – six women, one man – had cornered the television set at the far end of the ward. The patients were staring intently, listening to the news of the day being delivered by a zealously-cheerful, zealously-blonde TV Barbie. The news of the day was a stock market plunge. Behind the wheelchairs there was a row of armchairs whose backs were to the nursing station. Sitting in one of these chairs was a woman in a navy sweater and pink slacks and black knitted slippers.

Is this important? I think this is important.

She craned to her left, then her right, attempting to get a better view – between all the heads and the shoulders – of the television screen.

Move. I can't see.

Perhaps they heard her and perhaps they didn't but no one paid her any mind.

I think this is important. Is this important? I think I should be seeing this.

Lou was in the bed nearest the door of 211.

The fluorescent lamp over her bed was switched off. Aluminum safety rails had been raised on either side of the bed to keep her from rolling onto the floor. But just in case, a foam mat had been placed beside the bed, just under the rail.

Benjamin stood with his hands on the rail and leaned over for a closer look at Lou. She was wearing a salmon-coloured turban. Her head was turned from him. The bedsheets, blanket and comforter were pulled to her chin and held there by the arthritic fingers of her left hand. The fingers of her right were splayed across her face. Lou's skin seemed jaundiced, but it could have been the lack of light in the room. Judging by her breathing – soft, regular, slow – she was asleep. He spoke her name, just above a whisper, but did so only once and when she did not respond he pulled a visitor's chair to the side of the bed, removed his jacket and put it over the back of the chair and sat down.

Ten minutes past eight.

Between the bedside table and Benjamin's chair there was a roll-away eating table upon which there was a white Styrofoam drinking cup – plastic lid, articulated straw – three-quarters full of water; an opened but almost full eight-ounce can of chocolate-flavoured Ensure (complete balanced nutrition) and an apparently unread Sunday edition of The Minneapolis Star Tribune, with Lou's name written in black magic marker above the masthead.

Beyond Lou's bed, a privacy curtain had been drawn so that Benjamin could see neither the person in the neighbouring bed nor the view out the window. He could hear traffic whispering past on Lyndale Avenue and had no trouble hearing Lou's room-mate: every few moments she appeared to be choking to death. Then with great effort and much choking, wheezing, hacking and coughing – and the aid of a constantly-hissing ventilator – she managed to clear her throat. Then she fell silent again until the phlegm bubbled up in her wind-pipe, forcing her to fight once more for her life.

Wonderful advertisement, thought Benjamin, for the joys of smoking.

Beside this woman's bed, a radio was tuned to a golden oldies station: middle of the road fare these days – The Beatles, The Righteous Brothers, Buddy Holly – music the colour of nostalgia. It wasn't that long ago, he thought, that this music was the music of the fast lane, scandalizing parents and teachers and politicians. He remembered it well.

Even the lyrics.

That'll be the day-ay-ay that I...

That February day in 1959 Benjamin had been in the playground of West Hill Elementary when Norm Graham came running across the snow-covered baseball diamond, breathless with the news of the airplane crash. Benjamin's girlfriend, Donna Hartley, burst into tears and, before he quite realized what he was doing, Benjamin wrapped his arms around her and held her to his chest right there in the schoolyard not thirty yards from baggy-pants Mister Wilson. But Mister Wilson, ever watchful for the least infraction of the rules – and hugging your girlfriend was definitely against the rules – Mister Wilson, perhaps in a sorrow of his own, said nothing, not a word.

That night, side by side on the sofa in Donna's basement rec room, Donna's head on his shoulder, her hands sandwiched between his thighs, they played Buddy Holly's records over and over and over, fumbling into each other's clothes as that pure clear haunting southern voice haloed around them.

That was the late great Buddy Holly, folks. Don't go away. Right after these messages, we'll be back with six straight...

In the common room, the television was announcing a temporary halt in trading somewhere in the Far East. The woman in pink slacks was still asking those ahead of her to move so she could see the screen. A nurse was calling over the intercom for a Doctor Bailey. A woman in one of the nearby rooms was calling out: help, help, help. Oh God. Help, help, help.

God appeared to be momentarily distracted.

The woman beyond the privacy curtain began choking again.

Lou stirred: I hear pigeons.

Benjamin stood, leaned over the bed, put his hand on her shoulder.

Do you hear pigeons? she said. We should close the windows before they come into the room.

It's not pigeons, Lou. It's your neighbour, trying to breathe.

Lou opened her eyes and turned so that she could see the face belonging to the voice: Benjamin?

Hi Lou.

Benjamin leaned over the railing and embraced her, his right arm encircling her, his hand on her bare back where the hospital gown had separated. She put her left arm around his shoulder and pulled him close. He kissed her on the forehead. Then he stood beside the bed, holding her right hand in his.

How are the children?

The children were fine.

How's Kathleen?

Kathleen was fine.

Lou wanted details. Benjamin provided them.

Anna was in fourth year science, Aaron in second year philosophy, at university. They were working hard and doing fine.

Kathleen was working half-time which she enjoyed much more than working full-time. You can only take a classroom full of eight-year-olds, full-time, for so long before they check you into a padded room.

She's loving her time at home, said Benjamin. You know her: she's happiest when she's curled up on the couch reading her newspapers, reading her books, or playing the piano. And finally, she has some time to get back to the piano. It's a beautiful sound in the house again.

She has a lovely touch.

Yes, said Benjamin. She does.

And how are you?

Me? Fine. Couldn't be better.

How's your job?

Still better than working for a living.

Have you been travelling?

I was on the road for a couple of weeks. I was doing a profile of a rock and roll band for a magazine. So I followed them around from New York down to New Orleans then up to Louisville and back home. It was fun. But a couple of weeks on the road was enough for me. I think my road days are behind me.

How's Kathleen's mother?

Kathleen's mother was fine, as were Kathleen's sisters and brothers.

And their children?

And their children. And Benjamin spent the next few minutes providing details of all these various lives. Leaving out recent annoyances and irritations.

So everyone's well?

Everyone's well. Which brings us around to you. How are you doing?

Not well.

How are you feeling?

Not good.

What's the matter?

I'm tired, and I don't feel well.

You need to start eating something. It'll give you some strength and you'll start feeling better.

You sound like the nurses. Lou shut her eyes. But she didn't release her grip on his hand.

Did you have any breakfast?

She gave him the silent treatment.

The nurses said you didn't have any breakfast.

Lou opened her eyes. If you knew the answer, why ask the question? Thin smile.

Just thought I'd check.

Don't start treating me like a schoolgirl.

He smiled and gave her hand a squeeze. I'm worried about you. That's all.

There's nothing to worry about.

Starving yourself to death is something for me to worry about, he said.

She pulled her hand from his and tugged the covers up to her chin and shut her eyes.

Are you going to sleep?

She said nothing.

You want me to pull up the comforter?

Yes. Then, after a couple of seconds: please.

He pulled the comforter up over her shoulders.

I'll be right here. Benjamin sat in the armchair.

He glanced at his watch. Eight twenty-five. He leaned his head against the fingers of his right hand. Lou's breathing slowed and deepened.

Just like that, she was asleep.

Where do you go, Lou, when you drift off like that?

Lou was thinking of a photo – she still has it somewhere – showing her standing in the cemetery at Ephrata. She is standing a distance away from Mother, who has the camera, and is doing her best to remain still so as not to become a blur in the photograph. Standing still is not an easy thing to do when you are just two and a half years old.

In the photograph, Lou looks very elegant and grown-up: dress below the knees, fancy ribboned straw hat on her auburn hair. Very sophisticated. The photograph is very small – an inch wide by a couple tall – so it is not possible to see that Lou is very sad. She is sad, of course, because Father is not in the picture. Father is in the ground. Lou misses him already, although it's been only a week since they left the cemetery – Harry, Norman, David, Mother and Lou – leaving father behind.

Lou remembers thinking how lonely Father must be, deep in the earth, as the people he loved walk away and leave him behind. He could not see them, of course, but Lou imagined he could feel their footsteps receding in the distance.

Lou remembers walking very lightly on her tip-toes so as not to make him feel she was leaving him, so as not to make him feel any sadder than he already must feel, locked in a box, buried in the earth.

There would be times she imagined him calling out to her: she could hear him clearly, in that deep resonant voice, calling her name, pleading with her and the others not to go, not just yet, stay a little while longer before leaving him in this new and lonely place.

She remembers feeling very happy when they returned a week after the service – the day Mother had her pose for the photograph – came back and had a picnic lunch beside the grave, the earth still heaped up, wilting roses and carnations lying atop the dirt, that sunny Sunday. Lou remembers feeling less lonely herself, sitting on the grass beneath which Father lay.

They had come to Ephrata filled with fear and with hope.

Father had taken ill in New York, a cough deep in his chest, blood on the handkerchief he held to his mouth. The doctor said he couldn't tolerate the city air any longer, said he must leave the city and live in the country.

His lungs needed country air.

So they packed their things and took the train out of New York to Pennsylvania where Father had grown up, went back to the red brick house – verandah across the front and down one side – at Church and Main, the home in which he was born and raised, and moved in with his parents.

Had gone home in every sense that matters. But although Father did as the doctor ordered, sat in the Pennsylvania sunshine and breathed the Pennsylvania air and did not exert himself in any way, he did not get better. He became more pale by the day, and weaker, and Mother had to support him by the elbow when he rose from his chair and crossed the verandah and went back inside to the bed set up in the living room.

And then he died.

And even though they had buried him, saw the casket lowered into the ground, heard the prayers – May Light Perpetual Shine Upon Him – said over the grave; even though they had each thrown a handful of dirt down onto the lid of the casket, they could not quite believe Father was really gone.

Such a huge presence in their lives.

Such a huge absence.

There were times, sitting inside her Grandparents' house that Lou was certain she heard Father talking out there on the verandah, was certain he was out there talking with Mother in the fan-backed chairs set out in the sun.

Fingered the curtains back, to have a look.

Ephrata is a small place these days – twelve thousand souls – but it was much smaller then, of course, back just before The Great War.

But Lou remembers it as a large place: full of large white-painted houses and broad streets arched over with leafy maples and oaks. She remembers the sound of the place: dogs and birds, the clip and clop of the dairy-wagon horse, the wind in the trees. She remembers the sound of the skipping-rope slapping the sidewalk in front of her

Grandparents' house. She remembers her brothers' voices – Harry's especially : one thousand, two thousand, skip to my Lou, three thousand, four thousand, button your shoe.

Harry's voice. Harry's laughter.

Her lovely lost Harry.

His dark hair parted, just like Father's, a little to the left of center; his dark serious eyes; his solid Father chin, hint of a dimple.

She could feel his hand enclosing hers as they turned and left the graveyard that last time, the day they had to leave Ephrata and make their way back to New York, leaving Father behind, forever, in the ground in the country of his birth.

If you went to Ephrata today, you would most likely visit The Cloister. The Cloister was the home of the people who founded the town two hundred years before Lou was born. They were known as The Society of the Solitary Brethren. Lou loved the sound of the name of that little community. When she was a little older – and a long way from Pennsylvania – she fancied herself a member of that society; wondered, in fact, whether in a previous life she might have been one of the white-robed Virgins of the Solitary Brethren; felt that perhaps this had prepared her in some way for the solitary life she was about to endure.

Now and then, the Brethren came to visit her in her dreams – serious-looking folk in sandals and hooded robes who lived their simple lives in tune with the turning of the seasons, saying their prayers, counting their blessings, waiting for the end of this life and the start of the next.

She imagined them as dour people – serious at all times – hands stained from the earth which yielded their living. But when they beckoned in her dreams – arms outstretched toward her – she felt drawn to them in some comforting way; felt that if she could join them they would hold her in a loving embrace. But of course she could not join them. As soon as she tried – sitting up in bed suddenly awake in the middle of the night – they were gone.

The Solitary Brethren lived and worked in a community housed in stone-and-wood buildings, devoid of decoration. They slept on bare-board beds with a block of wood for a pillow, eschewing the comforts of this world while working to attain those of the next.

They rose early each morning and trudged out into the fields; ate simple meals of nuts and fruits and vegetables; prayed always and everywhere, slept five hours a night – rising at midnight to attend service; never ventured beyond the two hundred acres which they had carved out of the woods of Pennsylvania. And when they died they were buried in the cemetery at the edge of The Cloister, a cemetery now bordered by Main Street, a cemetery known as God's Acre.

Though Father was not buried in this cemetery, Lou came to call his cemetery God's Acre, too, and eventually took to calling all cemeteries by the same name.

She was thrilled when, years later, in school in Brooklyn, her teacher recited Longfellow's poem of the same name.

She memorized it and often found herself repeating its lines:

God's Acre! Yes, that blessed name imparts
Comfort to those, who in the grave have sown
The seed that they had garnered in their hearts,
    ....
Into its furrows shall we all be cast,
In the sure faith, that we shall rise again
    ....
This is the field and Acre of our God,
This is the place where human harvests grow!

This name brought her much comfort: made her feel as though her Father was not alone down there beneath the earth but was a part of a community of the quiet, quietly waiting in God's Acre for whatever might come next. So when she thought of Ephrata, all these other names sprang to mind: The Cloister, The Society of the Solitary Brethren, God's Acre. And Cocalico Creek, musical as its name, its glistening waters glinting through The Cloister and down into the town: the creek in which the faithful Solitary Brethren were baptized two hundred years before. In later years, though she never returned to the land of her Father's birth and death, Lou felt connected to that place as though it had been the land of her own birth. Whenever she thought of it, she thought of all those musical names and thought of her Father lying peacefully in the ground, his big carpenter's hands clasped over the vest of his charcoal Sunday suit, as though he were sleeping for a time before getting up and getting on with the remainder of his journey. And when she thought of him, as often she did in the years to come, the years when she was alone in the world, she felt less lonely and less sad.

She kept the photograph of herself – elegant and sad – taken that sunny day in God's Acre as a kind of charm: a charm which connected her to her own past, and that of her Father and his family.

Benjamin studied Lou's face.

Her lower jaw relaxed and fell, her lips receded into her open and toothless mouth. She looked, he thought, exactly as she would in a day or two, a week or two, when she breathed her last: looked just as she would when someone held her wrist, searching for a pulse, searching in vain before gently lowering the lifeless arm, pulling the sheets over her face.

Not a face you would want to remember.

Benjamin closed his eyes, conjured another face.

Lou's Christmas face, the red-eyed, tears-and-joy face that came smiling through the doorway of Gate Four at Metro Airport in Detroit, the Christmas after Bob died, the first of eighteen Christmas holidays Lou would spend with Kathleen and Benjamin and the children.

It was the first flight Lou had ever taken or, as she preferred it: the first time I've ever taken flight.

A face worthy of remembrance.

So, too, the face Benjamin encountered, coming down the stairs that first Christmas morning, Lou dressed and sitting in the dark before the still-darkened Christmas tree, awake before anyone else in the house, awake and waiting like a little girl, not wanting to miss a moment of any of this, her first Christmas with her new family.

So, too, the face which smiled across the silver-and-linen table for two at The Old River Inn where Benjamin had taken Lou for a special lunch (Lou having mentioned she would love to take a drive out of the city, see a bit of the rural Canada she'd heard so much about). Benjamin reserved a table by the window overlooking the Detroit River, ice-floed and sparkling in the mid-day sun. That luncheon had been all that Benjamin had hoped it would be and more than Lou had expected (and to which, over the years, she referred dozens of times). They had begun with cold soup – asparagus – and followed with pate and European breads accompanied by a glass of white wine (Lou's face flushing with the first few sips); they'd gone on to salmon (Lou) and steak (Benjamin) and more wine (chardonnay for Lou, merlot for Benjamin) and they'd followed this, European style, with salads and then dessert (cheese cake for her, Black Forest for him) from the trolley, followed by brandy and coffee.

The luncheon lasted until nearly four o'clock, until only the two of them remained in the dining room, half oblivious to the staff cleaning up and preparing for the first sitting of supper.

All this while they talked and talked, of his past and hers, of that time when she had first come into his life.

He'd asked about his parents and she'd played back the whole film.

Lou had taken an immediate liking to Benjamin's Mother. She was sweet, bright and down to earth. Benjamin's Father? He was bright. He was also big, brash and cocky. He was like a caricature of The American Baron of Business.

It had taken her a while to see it, or it had taken him a while to reveal it, but Benjamin's Father had another side: generous to a fault with those he liked, caring and considerate of friends and colleagues. But he could be, and often was, cool and distant with those he was still judging; cutting to those he deemed not useful; ruthless with those whom he disliked or distrusted or who found themselves in his path. He was not a man you'd want as your enemy, or your competitor. It was no surprise he terrified those who met him as he made the rounds of the factories whose owners had hired him to set things right, save the day.

Funny, then, to watch him dote on Benjamin's Mother, a woman who could make him dance like a marionette. All it took was a word – Luther – spoken in a certain tone of voice and Luther Miles would heel like a puppy.

They'd made quite a pair, Benjamin's Mother and Father. Lou remembered as though it were a photograph the first time she met them. They'd come west by train. Lou and Bob had been delegated to meet them at the station. Benjamin's Mother was first down the stairs of the railway car, the porter holding her hand until she alighted on the platform. Then Benjamin's Father had filled up the car's doorway, cane in one hand, bowler hat, black cape with red silk lining, matching rose in the lapel of his pin-striped double-breasted suit; had stood there for a moment, as though to be appreciated: Look, there's Clark Gable, a woman had said in passing. Apt comparison.

Luther Miles was a head-turner: six-two, built like a boxer (which he had been, in college) and like all men born with physical gifts, he knew how to play them like a trump card; knew how to enter a room, how to pause in a doorway just long enough to send a current through the room, how to turn himself out – wardrobe and deportment – in such a way that would encourage whispers, then silence, then smiles and nods; switching his cane to his left hand so as to free his right for the hands offered him as he mazed his way among the tables to the one reserved for him and his companions (always, of course, the best table in the house).

Lou wanted to know whether Benjamin remembered his Father's secretary: a man named Walter.

Benjamin didn't recall the name.

Walter Haggerty had been a wisp of a man. Looked like a secretary: wire-rimmed glasses, manicured nails, his shoulders always a little hunched as though he were carrying a heavy burden; his manner always just this side of obsequious. Walter made all the travelling arrangements for Luther Miles; made his appointments, got Luther into those places Luther wanted to get into and kept him out of places and away from people he wanted to avoid. Walter was a one-man retinue.

Luther was known to bark at Walter from time to time – goddammit Walter – but here was the telling of the tale: when Walter retired, Luther had all his bills – heat, hydro, telephone, taxes – routed to the office where they were paid promptly and in full and Luther kept Walter on the payroll, full salary, Christmas bonuses, annual increases, all the perks, until the day he died.

Luther Miles had been a ferociously loyal friend and repaid handsomely loyalty shown to him.

This was, of course, the same Luther Miles who thought nothing of firing a plant manager for an impudent word, a sneering glance.

Benjamin's Father had been, Lou thought, a sort of Jekyll and Hyde.

Which was, more or less, the way Benjamin remembered his Father as well.

Once, when they were living in the country, Luther decided he needed a fence to separate the remnants of an apple orchard from the remainder of the main yard. A fence six feet high and eighty feet long.

This, he said to Benjamin, is a post-hole digger. This is a shovel. This is a saw. And this is a hammer. I expect you can figure out how to make use of them.

That was it, for instructions.

Another infamous Luther test.

So, Benjamin set about digging the postholes. Eleven of them, eight feet apart.

It took him the better part of a week to dig the holes, mix and pour the cement, brace the poles, let the cement set. Then another week to assemble the frame and hammer the boards into place.

When he was done, he uncapped one of Luther's imported beers, something German and expensive, and sat in the sun, admiring his work.

It's not straight, said Luther, standing at the end of the fence and eyeing its length.

Not straight?

There, said Luther, pointing at the third post. That post is out of line.

Who cares? said Benjamin.

I care, said Luther.

Well, that makes one of us.

The one who matters, in this case, said Luther. You'll have to straighten it.

You can't straighten it, said Benjamin. Those posts are set in cement.

Benjamin looked at the fence.

Luther was right. The fence was out of line. By perhaps two inches.

Straighten it, said Luther.

I'll have to take it apart to straighten it.

I expect you will.

Why?

Because I'm telling you to.

And if I don't?

That's not an option.

It's my option.

No, said Luther. It's not. You built the fence. You built it carelessly and incorrectly and now you'll have to take it apart and start it again and do it properly.

No, said Benjamin, I don't. You asked me to build it. I built it. If you don't like it, you can...

And that was the first time, though not the last, that Luther had struck Benjamin: clipped him across the face with an open palm.

I won't stand for insolence. When you're living under my roof, you obey my rules, follow my instructions. And you never talk back. Ever.

And that was the first time, though not the last, that Benjamin had headed down the lane and down the road, knapsack on his back.

He was fourteen.

He could be such a bastard, said Benjamin.

Yes, said Lou. That he could.

These long and discursive trips into his past, with Lou as his guide, became one of the joys of Benjamin's adult life. Lou was the only person alive who could remember his parents from a time before he could remember them himself; was in fact one of perhaps a half dozen people on earth who could remember his parents at all. Lou was a kind of bridge to his past. A...

Would you like some flowers?

Hm?

Benjamin was startled by the visitor, was momentarily disoriented.

Checked the time.

Ten to nine.

The house-coated woman – short-clipped white hair, glasses which magnified her pale and watery blue eyes – was standing between Benjamin and Lou's bed, holding a fistful of sleepy-headed roses, their stems dripping water onto the tiled floor.

No, said Benjamin. Thank you very much. We've got some flowers. He pointed at the vase on the table beside Lou's bed, a vase containing Lou's sorry collection of asters and daisies.

You can never have too many flowers, said the woman. She extended the bouquet in his direction. Only a dollar. Benjamin moved his legs so the water from the flowers wouldn't drip onto his trousers. He reached out and gently pushed her hand to one side so the water dripped, once more, on the floor.

We have just the right number of flowers, he said. But thank you anyway.

I took these flowers from my dead friend's grave, said the woman.

Hm.

There you are. The nurse smiled down upon the diminutive flower lady. I've been looking for you, Mary.

Mary made as though she had not heard the nurse, turned to face the far end of Lou's room, intending perhaps to try to sell the flowers to Lou's gasping room-mate, struggling for breath on the far side of the curtain.

Not that way, Mary. Your room is this way.

Flowers? Would you like some flowers?

Those aren't your flowers, Mary. You've taken them from Conrad's room. Come along. We'll have to take them back.

The nurse reached for the flowers but Mary yanked her flower-carrying hand back, spattering water on Benjamin's face.

Oh, said the nurse.

Benjamin reached for a Kleenex. It's all right.

Come along, Mary. Conrad wants his flowers back.

He'll have to buy them.

No he won't. They're his flowers.

Flowers?

The nurse now had Mary by the elbow and was guiding her back toward the door.

If she comes back, keep an eye on your possessions. Someone has very sticky fingers. The nurse smiled an apologetic smile.

Benjamin nodded and smiled in return.

Come along, Mary.

Mary made a break for it, the nurse in pursuit.

The woman in the next bed was sputtering again.

An intercom voice announced: code alert, all clear. And repeated itself.

A janitor passed the door to Lou's room, pushing a wheeled bucket by the handle of the mop he'd stuck into the water. Benjamin could hear him, a moment later, as he squeezed the water from the mop, then slapped the mop against the floor.

Who was that?

One of your neighbours.

What did she want?

She wanted to sell us some flowers.

Did you buy them?

No. She'd taken them from someone else's room. The nurse came and took her away.

Oh, said Lou. Then: can you get me some water?

Benjamin put the straw to Lou's parched lips, then wiped her chin with a napkin. Can I get you anything else?

No.

Anything to eat?

No.

Anything at all?

No.

If I went out and bought you a piece of French silk pie, would you have some of that?

I might.

How big a piece would you like?

A regular piece.

Would you like it now, or later?

Now.

The weather had turned almost summery, an anomaly in Minnesota the last week of October. Benjamin put his leather coat in the trunk of the rented Olds, looked up at the sprawling cumulus clouds which zeppelined past the sun, shadowing the buildings – dentist's office, car dealership, Shell station – on the far side of Lyndale Avenue. When the clouds passed, Benjamin leaned his head back and closed his eyes against the brightness, relishing the warmth. He wondered whether he might not get the nurses to manoeuvre Lou into a wheelchair so he could wheel her out here into the sunshine; wondered whether feeling this warmth on her skin she might feel some reluctance about staying the course she'd chosen. But he wondered only briefly; got into the car and side-streeted his way from Lyndale to Penn, then south on Penn to the coffee shop where, once upon an earlier time, he would go first thing in the morning for his fix of caffeine and news of the day. He turned right at that corner and, several blocks down, pulled into the parking lot of Baker's Square where he bought a slice of pie which he carried out in its clear plastic container.

A few moments later, he was curbside in front of Lou's house – her former house – on whose front lawn stood a Century Real Estate sign across the upper corner of which someone had affixed a 'sold' sticker. The deal, negotiated at summer's end, was to close at the end of November. A young couple from Iowa had bought the place. They were expecting a second child and thought Lou's storey-and-a-half three-bedroom house would be perfect, after a little updating – plumbing and wiring. So Lou had chirruped on the telephone the day the deal had gone through.

I can only hope they'll be as happy in that house as we were though, quite frankly, I don't see how that's possible.

The lawn could have used some trimming, the gardens a good weeding. The yard man Lou had employed for years and years had finally quit, the arthritis getting the better of him. Neighbourhood kids, for a time, had relished the money, but not the work.

Benjamin parked in the drive.

He walked up to the living-room window and pressed close to the glass, palms cupped at either temple. The walls were discoloured where pictures had once hung; the broadloom dimpled where sofas and chairs had sat for years undisturbed. There were cobwebs in the upper corners of the walls beyond the fireplace. From where he stood, Benjamin could see through the living room to the dining room and, to the right of that, the hallway where the neighbour had found Lou not quite conscious, not quite dead. Benjamin had thought at the time the neighbour's intuition had been a fortunate thing, though he wondered whether Lou would now agree. Still, drifting into death, face down on the carpet of your own hallway, couldn't be a pleasant way to go.

Though who's to know?

If you were only barely conscious, it might be a little like drifting off to sleep.

Benjamin had had his own brush with death and hadn't noticed.

The summer he was seventeen he'd been plucked lifeless, limp and blueish from the bottom of a swimming pool in the south of England.

He'd been doing lengths – too many, too quickly – in the hope that two poolside brunettes would notice and admire him, invite him to join them for a drink and who knows what else. He chose the ladder nearest them to make his torsoed exit from the pool; grabbed a towel and began working on his hair (allowing the girls a moment to ogle when he wasn't looking). Then, starved for oxygen after the first strenuous exercise in years, he passed out and tumbled backwards into the pool, the towel still around his head.

His next conscious moment was looking up into the ruddy face of a bearded man giving him mouth to mouth.

When Benjamin sat up and looked around, the girls were nowhere to be seen. Benjamin's saviour couldn't say exactly how long he'd been at the bottom of the pool. He'd seen a group of people standing at the pool's edge, looking down and talking and when he joined them to see what they were looking at, he saw Benjamin down there on the pool's turquoise bottom. He asked the girls if their friend was just fooling around down there. They told him Benjamin was no friend of theirs. They didn't know who he was. They'd never set eyes on him before. When the man asked how long Benjamin had been down there, one of the girls giggled and said: oh, quite a few minutes now.

Benjamin's saviour was a Mister Arthur Edgerton. He was a retired teacher. He and Benjamin later corresponded for a number of years until one of Benjamin's letters returned, unopened, in an envelope containing a note informing him that Mister Edgerton had died.

The afternoon of the pool incident, which Benjamin had come to think of as the beginning of his second life, Mister Edgerton had joined him and his parents on the patio outside their cottage for drinks and hors d'oeuvres. Benjamin's parents were effusive in their thanks which – along with the offer of a monetary reward – Mister Edgerton brushed aside but nonetheless blushingly appreciated.

It's the first time I've saved anyone's life, he said, more than once.

When friends arrived for cocktails, Mother introduced Mister Edgerton, announced the news, encouraged Mister Edgerton to pick up the story, again.

Over supper – there was no question but that Mister Edgerton should join them – Mother declared there were a number of lessons to be learned from the afternoon's events. Benjamin should, thenceforth and evermore, be mindful of the power of the kindness of strangers. He should remember the dangers of vanity. And, said Mother, he would be well advised to think with his big head rather than his little one. Which advice sent Mister Edgerton into gales of laughter.

Benjamin would also be well advised to catalogue his strengths, weaknesses and limits of endurance; to contemplate the fragile and transitory nature of life and to appreciate his own life, while he still had it, in all its fullness and glory. That life would pass in the wink of an eye, relatively speaking, and once it was lived there would be no more evidence of it than there was evidence of this morning's foot-prints in the sand down there at the edge of the sea, whose evening beauty they were all now appreciating. Benjamin's Mother pointed her cigarette – in its onyx holder – in the direction of the boardwalk, by way of exclamation point.

His mother had been knee-deep in sand analogies that week, being knee-deep in Will Durant's hard-cover history of civilization.

Did you know, she said, that entire civilizations lie buried and lost beneath the sands of Africa? Civilizations which would put ours to shame. These brilliant people lived thousands of years before Christ; they had a sophisticated understanding of the universe and its laws, not to mention the follies and foibles and ways of man (at which point she looked over the rim of her gin and tonic at Benjamin). They built the most elaborate and breathtaking of cities, created the most sophis-ticated of societies; had all the comforts of our modern society, except for electricity and automobiles and their attendant evils.

She went on for several moments, rhapsodizing about attendant evils.

Benjamin was tempted to mention that, but for those evils, they would be back home in Canada tilling the soil behind a team of hors-es and churning their own butter by candlelight.

He also wondered, briefly, how Mister Durant could possibly know all this about people whose bones were buried beneath the dust and sand of Africa. However, he had the presence of mind not to say so, and instead poured Mother another gin and tonic.

Mister Edgerton raised his own empty glass when Benjamin came back to the table and by the time Benjamin returned with that drink, Mother had picked up the thread of the conversation regarding civilizations buried beneath the sands of time.

No matter how great your wealth (a look in Luther's direction), no matter how clever your schemes and designs, it can all be swept away in a moment. She snapped her manicured fingers. Just like that.

She stared intently at Benjamin, who was fixing himself a whiskey on ice. Something you should keep in mind. Particularly when you're older, she said. If you manage to get older. Which seems doubtful.

Close as he had come to dying, that brush with death was, strangely, almost an abstraction. Benjamin remembered only a brief sensation of dizziness after climbing from the pool; remembered thinking – at the moment of blacking out – that he should perhaps sit down and catch his breath; remembered nothing of his tumble into the deep end or his extrication from it.

No recollection at all.

He had wondered at the time, and again in the intervening years, whether he had been pulled back from his only chance at a painless death; whether his next death – the real one – would be agonizing in some unimaginable way. But he finally came to the conclusion that the first death, as he came to think of it, was a portent that he would drop one day like a stone, straight and silent into the depths and darkness (just as his parents were destined to do). Armed with this knowledge, he found himself able to live as few are able: beyond the shadow of the fear of death, a shadow which reduces others to cowering and cowardice.

He had come, in other words, to see his faux death as a blessing, a gift.

The incident in the pool effected other changes in him. He no longer considered random and accidental the apparently quirky tangents which life may take – such as the tangents in the lives of the characters of Father's much loved and talked-about novels of Mister Hardy. He came to believe that we come to the forks in the road and choose the paths we do because the path we choose will lead us into the life of a stranger at precisely the moment when such an encounter with that stranger is absolutely crucial, a matter of life and death.

Benjamin put great stock in the charity of strangers.

And he no longer saw the story of the Good Samaritan as a fable.

He also understood exactly why he picked up the telephone so many years before and dialed the number of a stranger in Minneapolis.

The alcoved back stoop of Lou's former house – between the garage and breezeway – was sheltered from the wind and cupped the sun. The thermometer – Bob had nailed it to the side of the garage so that Lou could see it from where she customarily sat at the kitchen table – read 71 degrees. Even so, the concrete step upon which Benjamin sat was still morning-cool.

In the yard to the south, beyond a fence which the neighbours had erected this past summer, there was a swing set: modern, made of plastic. In the yard to the north there was a wood-seat swing hanging from ropes looped around the limb of an oak. That swing had been there for thirty years or more; the branch was already growing around the ropes the first year Anna played on that swing twenty years earlier, the summer of their first visit. The neighbour – Audrey, the woman who had saved Lou's life – had told Benjamin he was free to bring Anna over any time he liked. It would be a joy to see a child on that swing again, so many years after her own children had grown and gone.

Beside the tree there was a sandbox and, in the garage, a box of shovels and pails and wooden toys which Anna could use as well. Audrey told Anna to help herself. You don't have to ask. Just make yourself at home. They had done just that. As Kathleen had said, the first night of their first visit: I feel at home here. It's strange, isn't it? Had been.

And yet Benjamin had felt the same. Though he could not remember Lou or Bob from the days of his childhood, Benjamin hadn't felt the slightest twinge of nervousness or apprehension driving across four states to meet them.

Weird, eh? Kathleen had thought. The last time you saw them, you were a little older than Anna is now. And the first time they met you, they were probably the age we are now.

Weird, too, but walking into their arms and lives had seemed to Benjamin the most natural thing in the world. He couldn't have explained why, but he felt then as he felt now, sitting on Lou's back stoop, that coming in to this house was, in some strange way, like coming home. In some peculiar way, he belonged; this was one of the places on earth – one of the very few – where he blended in with the background; where he fit; where he was safe, where the door – once closed behind him – kept the world at one remove.

For a long time after the death of his parents and the sale of their final home, this was the only place – apart from his own home – where he felt like that.

He had marveled more than once at the coincidence of all this: a phone call he could just as easily never have made; a visit he and Kathleen could have deferred until it was too late; a chance meeting of two people who had glanced through his life when he was a young-ster; a chance reunion just a year before Bob sat down in his living-room armchair, put the leg rest up, leaned back and drifted off.

Somehow, Lou had thought then, and many times since, it was des-tined that you'd come back into our lives.

It was a blessing.

Benjamin was put in mind of tangents, and strangers.

I'm not in the mood for any right now.

Benjamin held the plastic fork, heaped with chocolate custard pie-filling, a few inches from Lou's shrunken lips.

Looks pretty good, he said.

Maybe later.

He put the fork back in the container and closed the cover, put the container on the bed-side table beside the vase of flowers.

You were gone a long time.

He consulted his watch.

Quarter to ten.

Surprising, he thought, that she would have noticed the passing of time, drifting in and out of sleep, occupied with her wandering thoughts, wherever those thoughts happened to be wandering.

I stopped by the house.

What did it look like?

Forlorn. He described the look of the place, inside and out. I was looking for something that wasn't there.

What was that?

You, I guess. You and Uncle Bob. I was thinking about the kids, when they were young, playing on Audrey's swing, and in her sandbox. Those memories were so clear, and yet it's years ago, now. Twenty or more. All those years, gone in such a hurry. So I guess I went looking for all of us, back in those early years, when we first came out to see you.

A sentimental enterprise.

Lou turned her back to him, drew her knees toward her chest.

I was sitting on the back stoop. The new neighbours, the ones to the south...

The Arlingtons.

They've finished their fence. Looks nice.

When we moved in, there were no fences.

Benjamin recalled her telling him that, telling him you could go from one yard to another from one end of the block to the other. It was like a park back there when Lou and Bob moved in. The children ran and played, one yard to the next. No one minded. Even those, like Lou and Bob, who had no children of their own.

Lou and Bob loved sitting out in their yard, watching the children run this way and that, playing hide and go seek.

The children, in those distant days, used to scamper for the bushes and the garages. It was surprising how adept they were at crawling into places an adult would never think to crawl. All the while, the seeker with his hands over his eyes, calling out the countdown and then – ready or not, you're bound to be caught – running off in search of the hiders. Lou could hear them yet. And sure enough, someone couldn't help but laugh or giggle and give themselves away. And someone would always panic at the last second, leaving one perfectly good hiding spot in hopes of finding an even better one, and that person was inevitably the first to be caught.

I loved watching the children, Lou had said, and had said the same many times over down through the years.

The neighbourhood children played football and baseball out in those yards.

Once, a ball had come right through Lou's dining room window.

She and Bob had had some friends over for cocktails and bridge –

the Forsyths, you don't know them, they moved on before you came out for your first visit. Lou was just coming out from the kitchen with a tray of shrimp when the window exploded in front of her. The baseball landed at her feet in a glittering of glass. She remembered the look of horror on the face of the little boy who had thrown the ball. Little Willie Jensen – his parents lived four doors down.

Little Willie, when he'd let that ball fly, had been too astounded to move. And when it went crashing through Lou's window, he was stunned, just stood there, blubbering and wailing. His little friends lit off in six directions, but not little Willie Jensen. Little Willie just stood there with his baseball mitt on his hand and this mortified look on his face.

I'm thorry. I'm thorry. I didn't mean to do it. It wath an accthident.

Lou loved mimicking his missing-teeth lisp.

She and Bob and their guests couldn't help themselves. They started laughing. They told Willie it was all right, he hadn't hurt anyone. He could go home. They weren't going to call the police, have him thrown in jail.

I'm thorry. I'm thorry. I'll pay for the window. And off he ran, wailing and calling for his mother.

Do you remember Willie Jensen? said Benjamin.

Who? said Lou.

The little boy who threw the ball through your window?

Yes, said Lou. I think so. Why?

I was just thinking about him.

Sitting on the back stoop, I was thinking back to the sandbox next door. At Audrey's. Do you remember the sandbox? And the swing?

No response.

Anna used to love to play there. And Aaron, later.

Remember the big steam shovel Audrey had for her grandchildren? Anna and Aaron used to race each other to the sandbox to see who'd get to sit on it first. They'd play on that thing by the hour, shoveling the sand, spinning around, dumping it out.

Imagine, suddenly adults, when only yesterday they were babies.

Where do the years go? Hm?

Do you ever wonder about that, Lou?

Silence.

The days, said Benjamin, run away like wild horses over the hills.

That's a lovely line, said Lou.

It's not mine, said Benjamin.

It's a line from Charles Bukowski – title of a book, and a poem.

Lou had turned, opened her eyes. Was the rest of the poem as beautiful as the title? Lou smiled. And Benjamin realized it was the first time since he'd walked in and sat down that Lou had done that, had shown some of the old spark.

Parts of it – the parts I recall – were lovely. Most of it was about being out at the edge of the world, hanging on by your fingernails, getting drunk, chasing women.

How much of it can you remember?

Benjamin sat for a moment, dredging memory.

> There are times of thinking
> Of dead loves, dead flowers
> Of all the dead, dead people
> Who gave you a name

No, said Benjamin. That's not quite right. It's

> All the dead, dead people
> Who give you a name.

Cheerful, said Lou. Tell me more.

That's all I can remember, said Benjamin. I don't have much of a memory for poetry.

Which was not quite the truth.

Benjamin did remember more, quite a bit more – it being one of his favourite Bukowski poems – and all of it was strangely appropriate, given the circumstances. None of which he would recite for Lou, given the circumstances.

> The ugly duckling world
> Quietly slipping away from me
> And myself slipping away
> An old tiger
> Sick of the battle

Lou repeated the line about the horses. She had her eyes closed, then opened them again.

He was right about days, she said.

Yes, said Benjamin. He was right about days.

Lou was thinking of a distant day – 1920, summer, in a park in Brooklyn. It was a Sunday in August and they had walked to Sunset Park – 44th and 5th – after church.

Lou had a snapshot in one of her albums – where were her albums? – taken that day in the park: Harry taking the snapshots one after the other – don't waste all the film, Harry! – as though to freeze and preserve his subjects: Mother and Lou, Norman and David, and thus prevent further vanishings.

In the snapshot, Mother is leaning against a bouldered wall in an ankle-length dress. She is wearing a straw hat, with a ribbon around its crown.

The snapshot is in black and white.

Lou's memory is full of colour: Mother's dress is pale blue – the colour of the sky – with navy piping at the throat, matching the navy ribbon on her hat.

Lou's dress is pink. She is wearing white stockings and red slipper shoes, the kind with a strap around the ankle. She is wearing no hat (the better to display her wealth of auburn hair).

Lou is leaning against Mother, whose left arm is around Lou's waist.

Look over there.

Harry had them look to their left, so that in the snapshot it seems they had just seen someone, or were expecting someone they knew to walk in to the park and join them.

In reality, they were watching Norman and David who sat on a low stone wall a little distance away, shoes and stockings off, Sunday trousers rolled up to the knee, bare feet in the water of the duck pond, throwing bread crumbs and hoping for the best.

Lou can still remember the warmth of Mother's arm around her waist, and can still faintly detect Mother's perfume which made her think – then, as now – of white flowers in a green meadow.

Lou was eight the year Harry took that photograph.

Mother would be dead within the year.

Her Mother dead and Lou and the boys scattered like so much dust on the wind.

When she thinks of that day in the park and the weeks and months which followed – the final few – she wonders if they made some kind of mistake, all of them. Took a wrong turn, a wrong path which led to such disaster and sorrow.

She wonders whether – if they had chosen another way, had stayed in Ephrata, perhaps, stayed with Father's people, things might have turned out differently; wondered whether – if they had not left Father behind – they might have been spared.

But, of course, that could not have been: Mother couldn't stand to be in the same house with Father's Father; the resemblance was unnerving, strong enough to make her shudder every time Grandfather walked in through the door or down the stairs.

It would have been like living with a ghost.

Two ghosts, actually: Father not far away, resting in the ground in God's Acre.

So they packed up and went back to New York.

We'll be fine.

You'll see.

But despite Mother's wan smile and words of assurance, there was no force of conviction in either word or smile.

She had known, perhaps, that it was a faint hope; too faint to carry them all to safety.

Shall we have some lunch?

Lunch? Norman said.

Yes, said David.

I'm starved, said Harry.

And so – that fair summer Sunday in the final year of her life, Mother led them out of the park, Lou holding one hand, David the other, Harry and Norman bringing up the rear, out of the park on a path whose end point none of them could have imagined.

Benjamin, too, was thinking.

He was thinking of a day nearly thirty years before.

Hello, Benjamin. It's Father.

No mistaking that resonant voice. But the tone was new. Some kind of uncertainty. Some kind of hesitation.

When did you last see Grady?

I don't know. Benjamin had turned to Kathleen: when was Grady here?

Five months ago. Five or six. November, wasn't it? November I think. Why?

November, we think. Why?

The police are looking for him.

The police?

The police? Kathleen dropped the newspaper on her lap. She was all ears now.

In Vancouver.

Vancouver?

Kathleen couldn't take this: got up from the living room sofa and headed up the stairs to the bedroom and the other extension.

They seem to think he may have been murdered.

Murdered?

Someone has apparently come forward, has told the police he over-heard people talking about a killing. He mentioned Grady's name. It's all very vague. This person, whoever it is, is known to the police. He isn't known to be all that reliable. Nevertheless...

What else did the police say?

They said they were just following up; that once this informant mentioned Grady's name they were obliged to check things out, see if there's anything to what he's saying. So they're trying to track Grady's movements, see if anyone has seen him. They're trying to see if there's any substance to what this fellow is saying.

What is he saying?

He said he heard there was a dispute of some kind – something to do with drugs, or stolen goods – and that Grady was involved. Owed money to someone, refused to pay. Or couldn't pay. Or hadn't paid.

Someone killed him over a bad debt?

The police seemed to indicate it was more than a bad debt. It seems he had fallen in with some very unsavoury people. People it's best not to deal with, especially not to owe money to. November, you say?

Yes, said Benjamin. I think so. He called late at night – the usual scenario – then came over the next evening for supper.

The usual scenario was a late-night call – Grady drunk, Grady gone all sentimental, Grady suddenly feeling the need to hear his brother's voice.

We're Miles. We've got to stick together. We're brothers.

They were, after a fashion.

Benjamin was fifteen the summer he learned he had a brother.

Half brother, Mother insisting, hoping to maintain whatever distance was possible, as much distance as was possible, for as long as possible.

Grady had pulled into the drive of their country home in a silver Porsche coupe one winter's day in 1960. Stepped out looking like a million bucks in his knife-pressed slacks and gleaming loafers and camel-hair coat; had circled the car and opened the passenger door, offered his hand to a stunning someone, helped her out of the low-slung car.

Benjamin had been watching, wide-eyed, from the living-room window; opened the front door just as the chimes sounded.

Your Father isn't here.

Benjamin had been startled by Mother's voice, had not heard her come up behind him, turned and saw – that daggered look – that Mother had not been talking to him, but to this smiling, dimpled, well-dressed, handsome young man standing on the front porch, a beautiful woman on his arm.

Mother pulled Benjamin back a step and then gently shut the door.

Who was that?

That was your Father's son.

Son? He's my brother?

It's a long story. Ask your Father.

Luther – that evening – had been sparing with the details. Many years earlier, living in California, Luther had married. The marriage hadn't lasted, hadn't lasted long. Grady stayed behind with his Mother when Luther left, and left the state.

What's he do?

Luther didn't know.

He must have a good job. He was driving a Porsche.

He always liked the finer things, said Luther.

Whether or not he could afford them, Mother offered, over her shoulder.

Was that his wife?

Luther didn't know. He hadn't seen Grady in some time.

It wasn't the wife he had the last time we saw him, Mother said. Or the wife before that.

How did he seem?

Seem?

When you saw him, in November.

Fine, said Benjamin. Same old Grady.

Grady arrived at their apartment looking, as usual, like a million: very conservative grey suit, plain, no stripes, button-down white shirt and blue-and-red striped tie – always a Windsor knot – and those impeccable shoes, gleaming brogues.

He shed the jacket, loosened the tie, rolled up his sleeves and head-ed for the kitchen.

There's only one way to make a Bloody Mary.

And had demonstrated.

And demonstrated.

And, just past midnight – just one more for the road – he made his pitch: could Benjamin help him out? Cash a cheque for a couple of hundred?

No, Benjamin said. No, he couldn't. Benjamin reminded Grady about the difficulty with the last cheque.

Some confusion at the bank, Grady said.

No, said Benjamin. There'd been no confusion at the bank. They were quite clear: you no longer had an account at that bank.

Yes, well. Let's let bygones be bygones. We can't let these little…

No, Grady. No more cheques. I told you the last time. The last time was the last time.

Grady made one of his famous fluttering motions with his left hand – diamond ring glinting – well, can you let me have twenty dollars. Until the next time.

Benjamin went to the closet, pulled twenty from the wallet in his suit jacket.

Grady smiled a dimpled smile, patted him on the shoulder.

How be you try to make a Bloody Mary that's half as good as the ones your big brother can make. Hm?

Benjamin ought to have known better.

Next morning, on his way downtown to do errands, he pulled the wallet from his suit jacket and knew, even before he opened it, what to expect.

Grady had left a ten-dollar bill and taken the rest. More than a hundred.

Wrapped around the ten was a scrap of paper: thanks for the loan. You know I'm good for it. I'll pay you back with interest.

Bastard.

He seemed fine, said Benjamin. Normal.

Benjamin omitted the details of their last financial transaction.

Well, said Luther, if you hear from him, let me know.

Yes, said Benjamin. I will.

They both held the receivers to their ear.

Dad?

Yes.

How are you doing?

Fine, said Luther. I'm fine.

You want me to come home for a day or two?

No, said Luther. No, there's no need for that. There's nothing to be done. We'll just have to wait and see what the police turn up. I'll keep you informed.

What the police turned up – just about exactly where their informant had told them to look – in a firepit in a clearing in a forest north of Vancouver – was Grady's skull, bullet hole in the forehead, and buried nearby his clothes and his bones.

Lou was snoring.

Benjamin checked his watch.

Twelve past ten.

Benjamin patted Lou on the shoulder, adjusted the comforter so she would not be chilled, then got up and left the room.

Out in the common room, the old women were semi-circled in front of the television though it did not seem many were actually watching the screen. He negotiated a flotilla of wheelchairs, smiled at the nurse behind the counter, and walked down the corridor.

Beside the doors leading to each of the patient rooms there were glass-fronted display areas where framed photographs of loved ones were propped on the shelves. In some of these, children had left stuffed toys and notes to grandparents: in one there was a hand-crafted Valentine card: Granny I Love You.

Half-way down the corridor, there was an alcove with armchairs facing the two elevator doors. Two men sat staring at the doors, as though waiting for them to open and some familiar someone to step out and step back into their lives. They looked up and regarded Benjamin with expressionless stares.

Both elevators were on the ground floor.

The world's slowest elevators, said one of the men.

But in here, said the other, who cares about speed? What else we got to do, but wait?

The first man nodded in agreement, and they both turned again to look at the elevator doors.

Benjamin decided to take the stairs.

He tried the handle of the door around the corner, but the door was locked. There was a punch-pad beside the door, but he didn't know the code.

It's the year, smirked an orderly. If you know what year it is, you're a free man. If not, you get to stay with us.

Benjamin punched the numbers and was a free man and took the grey-painted stairs one flight down to the lobby.

And going down the stairs he recalled, for no reason he could think of, a news story he had heard on the radio while driving home one evening the previous week.

Three fishermen had got themselves stranded. They'd been out in Rondeau Bay, off Lake Erie, cut their engine, tossed in their lines and sat there, bewitched by a fair wind and a sunny day, sat talking and fishing.

Next thing they knew, that fair wind had pushed them toward shore and grounded them up on a mudflat in the middle of the bay. They were stuck, a mile from dry land. The outboard was useless, the propellor down in the mud. They tried pushing themselves free with the oars, but it was no use. They were stranded by their own weight. One moment, they were in good water. Next thing they knew, a fair wind had betrayed them, left them standing in their own boat, waving their arms, hollering for help.

Benjamin opened the door, leading to the lobby.

He was thinking of the old boys, sitting in the chairs by the elevator, and the old women sitting in their wheelchairs by the television, and Lou in her bed.

Beached, all of them.

Beyond help or hope.

In the lobby there were four armchairs side by side facing a bird cage which occupied the entire wall facing the entranceway to the building, so that it was the first thing you would see upon entering.

The cage was about ten feet tall by thirty wide and six deep. Inside, dozens of birds: birds on branches, birds in straw nests, birds pecking for food on the floor of the cage. Some of the birds were singing, some silent. One, with its head tucked under its wing, seemed to be sleeping.

When Lou first moved in, she loved to come down to the lobby to watch the birds. It reminded her a little of home. In the alcove between the garage and her kitchen window she used to keep a feeder so that, while having her coffee in the morning, or her lunch at noon, she could watch the birds outside the window. Sparrows and chickadees, finches and jays. She could watch by the hour. Sitting in front of the bird cage she could transport herself out of the lobby and into another place and time. Its intended purpose. She thought perhaps the birds were thinking the same thoughts.

Lou asked Benjamin if he knew the names of the birds in the cage.

That one's a finch, I think.

Yes.

And that one's a sparrow.

No, said Lou. That's a chickadee. That one, up there – she pointed at the upper right corner of the cage – that's a sparrow. Can you tell the difference?

Yes, he said, though he wasn't certain he could tell them apart if they flew around and landed in a different place.

Lou went on to name the birds in the cage: kinglets and grosbeaks, finches and wrens, warblers and nuthatches.

Aren't you interested in birds?

I like to hear them sing.

You ought to take a greater interest in the world which surrounds you, Benjamin. It's a world full of wonders.

So I've heard.

She turned, caught him smiling, slapped him lightly on the arm. You should. I'm serious.

She was serious.

And she had taken an interest in the world around her.

She had a memory like a razor: she could remember the names of the theatres (The Tivoli, The Grand, The Fox) where she and Robert had gone in New York; could name the movies they'd seen in each (Casablanca, and others). She could even remember some of the newsreels they'd watched before the main features and thus could remember the month, or at least the year, when they'd watched those movies. She could remember, in some instances, the names of the restaurants where they'd dined before or after those long-ago movies; could remember not just what she had eaten, but what Robert had eaten as well, what he'd had for dessert.

Of course I'm cheating. He only liked half a dozen desserts.

Benjamin wondered more than once how she managed to remember all those details.

I paid attention at the time.

Paid attention at the time?

That's why we're here. To pay attention. See what surrounds us.

Which was one of Lou's secrets for successful living.

So many people don't pay attention. They go places, do things, say things, hear things, see things, and none of it registers. Ask them five days later where they were last Monday and they won't be able to tell you. Ask them five minutes later what they've just seen, or heard, and most people will have a tough time answering.

Most people, she thought, go through life like they're half asleep. They only think they're awake, but in fact they're sleep-walking.

Lou told him of a time when she visited the Metropolitan Museum of Art in New York. She'd been mesmerized by Manet's painting entitled Boating, an oil depicting a man and a woman in a sailboat, the man at the tiller, the woman to his right. In the painting, the man is looking past the woman and she is looking across the boat at the horizon. Lou had spent half an hour wondering what those people had been talking about, wondered what had happened in their lives that had left them both in such a profound silence on such a warm and beautiful day. Although the painting was infused with light – the man in white, the water dappled and sparkling – it was, Lou thought, a very dark picture, very dire. She had the sense that this couple had come upon hard times, had perhaps come to the end of things; sensed that perhaps this was their final day together, that perhaps after this sunny afternoon on the boat they would be forced by circumstances to go their own separate, unhappy and unfulfilling ways – perhaps destined to return to their own spouses. The longer she sat in front of the painting, the more endings she could imagine for this story.

For the last few minutes observing the painting, Lou noticed a man standing to the left of her, also looking at the painting. When she turned to leave, he turned and followed, a step or two behind.

At the doorway of the gallery, she stopped and turned, asked him what he thought of the painting.

Painting?

The Manet. Boating.

Boating?

Lou pointed in the direction of the painting.

Oh, he said. Yes. Lovely.

He hadn't seen the painting at all. He may have been looking at it, but he certainly hadn't seen it.

Which was just one of the things which drove Lou to distraction when she went to art galleries.

Do you know how long people spend, on average, in front of a painting in a gallery?

A minute, guessed Benjamin. Two?

Three seconds, said Lou. Someone actually observed them, timed them with a stopwatch. Three seconds. Not even time to look from the top left corner to the bottom right. Stop, gawk, move on.

If someone was going to spend a week or a month creating a painting, was it really too much to ask that someone spend half an hour looking at it, studying it, reading it, thinking about it?

People are in such an unholy rush. Go here, go there, look at this, taste that, listen to this, see you later. They don't give themselves time to concentrate on any one thing for more than a minute or two before rushing off to the next thing. They never stop long enough to draw breath, never mind open their eyes and their ears. Is it any wonder no one can remember anything of value?

We've lost that ability, most of us, by the time we become adults. People are always amazed that, years later, they can remember the things they did as a child. That was no secret, no mystery, Lou thought. Children have the gift of concentration. When they listen to music, they really listen. When they watch the stars, they flop on their backs and stare. Really stare. When they study ants, they're flat on their bellies, their nose an inch from the grass. Full of wonder and awe. They see things – stars or ants – in such a way as never to forget. They see with intensity. Is it any wonder that eighty years later, they will see those stars – or those ants in the grass – precisely as they saw them when they were ten? It wasn't that people's memories failed them, Lou thought. It was just that most people, somewhere along the way, had lost that child-like ability to live directly in the center of their world, the centre of their own lives. She, for some reason or other, had retained it.

Further proof, Benjamin said, that you never grew up.

I suppose, said Lou.

You should pay attention, Benjamin. Really pay attention. See what you're looking at. Hear what you're listening to. Feel what you're touching. Yes, he said. I will. I take the pledge. He raised his right hand. I, Benjamin Miles, do hereby swear and signify that henceforth and furthermore…And it had seemed a good idea at the time: to wake up to the world around him. He should be more aware of the birds. He ought to be able to tell an oak from an ash. He ought not to be walking around semi-conscious through all these sights and sounds and wonders.

Not long ago – a month, perhaps less – Benjamin had been at a meeting and while waiting for others to arrive, the woman beside him had turned and said: it's a great day to be alive.

Yes, Benjamin said. I guess it is.

You shouldn't have to guess, said the woman.

Another overly-intense crackpot, he thought, smiling at her all the while.

You never know, she said. It could be your last.

Hm.

And she went on about the need to live each day as though it were your last.

In fact, she'd signed up for a course wherein the participants all agreed to spend the following year as though it were the final year of their lives.

They met once a month and went through exercises designed to force them to deal with something they'd all been accustomed to ignoring: the fact of their own impending death. Whenever that might be.

Hm, said Benjamin.

That was roughly my reaction when a friend told me about it, said the woman. I was skeptical, too. Sounded way too touchy-feely for me. But it's been fabulous. We're only four months into it and already...

And she might have gone on to explain in greater detail but the chairman, at that moment, cleared his throat and got the meeting underway.

All through the meeting, Benjamin found himself thinking about what the woman had said and when the meeting adjourned – he couldn't say, later, exactly what people had been talking about, what had been decided if anything – he wanted to ask the woman to tell him more about her courses, but she was leaving the room with some-one else and he missed his chance.

On the way home, it was all he could think about.

The last year of your life.

Could be.

And if it wasn't, one of these years certainly would be.

Which got him wondering about the passage of time.

He remembered once, when he was just a boy – eight or nine – his Mother had some friends over for a game of bridge. She asked him to bring a tray of cookies from the kitchen. Just as he set the tray down on the table, his Mother said to one of her friends: I remember – it must be twenty-five years ago...

That sentence stopped Benjamin in his tracks.

He couldn't imagine the passage of twenty-five years.

Twenty-five years seemed to him an eternity.

And now, here he was – forty years later – remembering his Mother talking about remembering something twenty-five years before that.

He could remember that moment as clearly as though she had uttered the words just days before.

And she'd been dead for nearly thirty years.

Those years seemed to have passed in a kind of blur. Which made him wonder: if nearly fifty years of my life can go by in such a blur, how quickly will the next few disappear?

How many more years might he be allotted?

Ten?

Twelve?

Fifteen?

He thought back ten years – to the days Aaron was playing baseball. He tried to recall the years which had followed. He could remember signal moments – certain assignments he'd had, Anna's graduation from high school, then Aaron's, but the rest of those years – what had happened during them, what had happened to them? If those years could just vanish, how quickly would his remaining years do the same? And if those ten years could pass so fleetingly, what of his remaining years? If he had ten years left – which may be wishful thinking – how quickly would they pass? How should he spend them, those last few precious years of his life?

He thought of an hourglass. He would like to have imagined a little more sand at the top. And he'd like what little was left to drain a little more slowly.

He thought he should follow that woman's example: live life a little more attentively. Consider this as perhaps the last year of his life. Live that year as intensely as he could. Make a point of living in the present tense. Make the most of the time he might have left. Pay attention to the world around him, appreciate the sounds and sights and delights of the world in which he found himself. Learn the names of birds. Learn the names of flowers. Be alive. Truly alive. While you could.

So much for good intentions. He'd gone right back to his old ways. Though he did like to listen to the birds – whatever they were – as he took his daily walks.

And he enjoyed listening to them now as he walked twice around the block to get some fresh air, an antidote to the smells and the sounds of the ward in which Lou lived.

The elevator door opened.

The same two men were there.

They did not seem to recognize him.

Benjamin walked down the corridor, through the common room and back to Lou's room.

Ten fifty eight.

Someone had set a food tray beside Lou's unread newspaper.

Lunch consisted of a cup of coffee (black, still steaming); two beet slices on a limp leaf of lettuce in a shallow dish beside a plate covered with a maroon-coloured plastic lid which Benjamin lifted to reveal one chicken leg, skin removed, a plop of mashed potatoes over which was poured a yellowish gravy which puddled on the plate around it; thirteen yellow beans (warm, but overcooked and spongy). Benjamin replaced the cover. There was also an eight-ounce carton of two-percent milk, a tiny cup of ice cream and one napkin, stained with the coffee which had slopped from the cup when the orderly had plunked the tray on the table.

Lou?

Lou slept on.

Your lunch is here.

Lou didn't stir.

There's chicken and some…

He went through the menu, trying to make the meal sound more enticing than it looked.

Can I feed you a bit of lunch?

Apparently not.

Do you mind if I have the coffee?

Lou sighed, shifted a little, slept on.

Where are you now, Lou?

Lou was in the apartment in Brooklyn. It was a two-bedroom walkup on the third floor of a building at 48th and 4th.

The building was made of brown brick and had double front doors, brown paint peeling, at the top of a steep cement stair. Inside, it smelled of dust and mould and whatever the neighbours happened to be cooking. The neighbours, in Lou's memory, seemed to have a preference for cabbage and sauerkraut. The stair leading from the lobby was steep and narrow, the stairwell poorly lit – when lit at all – by single bulbs hanging from ceiling wires. On the way up or down you could hear the voices of the tenants through the thin walls.

Their apartment was near the end of the corridor on the third floor: apartment 5. The front door opened onto a living room whose two windows – opposite the front door – gave on to the alley at the back of the building opposite. There were windows in that wall as well. An old man lived in the apartment opposite theirs and could be seen, day and night, moving about his apartment in trousers, undershirt and suspenders. He didn't seem to notice – or to care if he did notice – that Lou and the others could see him plain as day. He rarely looked their way. Once, though, he noticed Lou sitting in the chair by the window and he smiled in her direction, gave her a slight wave of the hand. She hadn't known what to do in return, so she just sat there and he turned and went about his business.

The kitchen and the bathroom were to the right of the front door; the two bedrooms to the left. Lou and her Mother shared the bedroom nearest the alley – two more windows – the boys shared the other; a single bed and a double. Harry, because he was the oldest, had his own bed. Lou shared the bed with her Mother.

The apartment was rarely quiet. You could hear noises from the street – automobiles and the shod hooves of the horses which still, in those years at the beginning of The Great War, pulled the carts and wagons from place to place in the borough. Within the building: voices from the apartments adjacent to theirs, footsteps and slammings elsewhere.

Their furniture was basic: beds and bureaux; a couch and a low table before it; an armchair and hassock and, in the corner of the living room, the dining-room table which had been in the dining room of their first apartment, the one they had all shared, a table around which they had all sat for their evening meal.

Lou's Mother was an indifferent cook: by the time she got home from wherever she had been cleaning that day she was too worn and weary to attempt anything but potatoes and vegetables and a bit of meat of some kind – beef or chopped meat. Sometimes days went by when their only meal was potatoes, boiled or mashed.

Since Father died, it was all Mother could do to pay the rent and buy the basics.

Lou was dressed, always, in her Mother's clothes, cut and adjusted to fit.

Harry had grown into some of Father's clothes and wore Father's shoes and boots although they were a size too large: the effect of which was to make him sound as though they weighed too much as well.

The younger boys dressed in whatever Mother could find at a reasonable price and in good condition at the second-hand shop on Fifth Avenue.

Since Father died, the four of them – Lou and the boys – were often alone in the apartment: Norman, David and Lou after school; Harry coming in from his job at The Hardware.

Mother rarely came home before six, sometimes as late as seven if she happened to be working that day over in Bay Ridge or in Flatbush.

Lou's memory of her Mother in those years in Brooklyn was of a woman at the last extremity of her resources: her hair always seemed dishevelled when she got home, her clothes always damp with perspiration – winter and summer – from the long day at work and the long journey home, foot and trolley.

It was not unusual for Mother to come in the door, drop her coat on the arm of the chair and go directly to her bed. Many the morning Lou woke to find Mother beside her, still in the clothes she had worn to work the day before.

On those days when Mother was late, Harry took to the kitchen and prepared something for them to eat and so it was he had become a passable cook.

And on one such day, in the year Lou turned nine, Harry had cooked, had supervised the baths, had seen them all to bed and then had sat up reading Oliver Twist, Harry loving the stories of Dickens – waiting for Mother to come home. When Lou woke in the morning – alone in bed – and went out to the living room she found Harry asleep on the couch, still in his clothes, the book spine-up, splayed on his chest.

They hadn't known what to do. Mother had never before failed to come home.

Perhaps, thought Norman, she had had to work late and had missed her trolley and decided to sleep over at her employer's, although she had never done any such thing before. Perhaps she had taken ill, thought David. Perhaps she was in a hospital somewhere. Maybe they should go to the hospital and ask after her. Lou hadn't known what to think.

Harry consulted Mother's handwritten schedule of work: days and locations. Said he would take the 3rd Avenue trolley out to Bay Ridge, to the place she had worked yesterday. That place, then the one she was scheduled to clean today. He would find her. They weren't to worry. They should go off to school and try not to worry and he would be home – he and Mother – when they returned from school. Which turned out not to be the case.

Norman, David and Lou returned to an empty flat. Not knowing what else to do, they sat on the couch and stared at the locked door and waited for the sound of Harry's boots on the stair.

Instead, there was the sound of two sets of boots and then a knock.

And then two more knocks.

Who is it?

The Police.

The Police turned out to be two officers – one young, one in whiskers – who wanted to know if they were alone. They told the officers about Harry – that he had gone in search of their Mother who had not come home the night before. The officers looked at each other and then at the children, wanted to know when Harry might be home. They told the officers Harry said he'd be home – Mother, too – when they returned from school.

I see, said the older officer.

Well, said the younger, we'll just wait with you until he comes, then. And the two officers took a seat on the couch, hands folded in their laps, all five staring at each other for what seemed an awfully long time. I can make tea, Norman said, and the tea was steeping when they heard footsteps in the hall and then the sound of Harry's key in the lock of the front door.

Harry looked at the officers – both of whom had stood and were holding their caps in front of them – then looked at the children, then back at the officers.

They haven't been in trouble, have they?

No, said the younger officer.

May we have a word with you in private, son? said the other.

And they had gone into Mother's room – Mother's and Lou's – and had shut the door.

And Lou could hear Harry's awful sobbing as clearly now as when she heard it that evening in Brooklyn eighty-three years ago.

Benjamin cradled Lou's coffee cup between both hands, crossed his legs at the knee, stared at the back of Lou's head.

He raised the cup, sniffed the coffee.

At Lou's house, the coffee was always on. She made half-pots – couldn't stand burnt coffee – and plenty of them. From the time she woke until the time she watched the evening news with Walter Cronkite, there was a mug not far from the tips of her fingers. She kept tins of coffee in the basement, as though fearful that one morning she might wake up and find herself looking at the bottom of the last empty canister. She was addicted to coffee the way some people are addicted to cigarettes.

When they came down in the summer to help Lou clean out the house, Kathleen took the main floor detail – helping Lou sort through file folders and clothes closets and kitchen cabinets – and Benjamin headed for the basement.

Take anything you want, said Lou. Throw the rest.

Benjamin yanked the string of the overhead light in the center of the basement and found himself staring at a wall of shelving filled, one end to the other, top to bottom, with canned goods and paper goods.

It looks like a grocery store down here, Lou. Do you have any idea how many tins of coffee you have?

Two or three?

There were eleven one-pound cans of Folgers coffee, shoulder to shoulder, on the shelf.

Which wasn't the half of it.

There were tins by the dozen: vegetables and soup and fruit. There were jars of pickles and jars of olives. There were boxes of cereal and bags of flour and sugar. There were five shelves of Kleenex boxes and paper towels and toilet paper. There were jars of Javex and box after box of laundry detergent.

It was a one-person grocery store.

You've got enough stuff down here to keep you going through a fairly lengthy war.

Bob liked to take advantage of sales.

Bob?

Bob had been dead for nearly twenty years.

Yes, well. It kind of rubbed off on me, I guess.

I guess.

Bob and Lou, and later Lou alone, loved to peruse the foodstore flyers then they (later she) would make the rounds, store to store, rack of specials to rack of specials. It was Bob's philosophy and policy never to pay full price for anything and to stock up on everything that was a bargain. Or close to a bargain. A penny saved and so forth.

What are you going to do with all this stuff?

You could take it home with you, if you want.

We brought a car, Lou, not a transport truck.

Benjamin took the coffee – there were still ten tins of Folgers on the shelves in their basement back home in Canada – and helped carry the rest, box by box, bag by bag, up the stairs and into the van sent by the Mission For The Needy.

There should be some nice tools down there.

There had been and a box of them – screwdrivers and files, wrenches, a drill, a sander, a square, two saws, a hammer and who knows what else – had found their way to Benjamin's basement as well. Though in his basement, they were piled on the counter in his workshop: no neat pegboard such as the one Bob had erected across one wall of the basement, a place for everything and the outline of the tool painted on the pegboard to ensure that each made its way back to its proper place after being used.

What'll we do about the washer and dryer?

They'll go in the auction.

Remember when we went out and bought them?

That would have been the summer after Bob died, the summer Kathleen and Benjamin and the kids had come to spend a couple of weeks with Lou; help her tackle Bob's room and his books and his papers; clean up the yard, paint the trim of the house, make themselves useful, keep Lou company, in those early lonely days.

Lou and Bob had never owned a washer or a dryer, which Kathleen and Benjamin had discovered that first visit when – armload of laundry – Kathleen had wondered if she could put in a load.

Oh, said Lou. We go to the Laundromat. Just down the street.

How on earth have you managed all these years without a washer and a dryer? Kathleen had wanted to know.

Lou had never really thought about it. Or so she said. She and Bob made their weekly trips to the Laundromat; loaded the machines, sat side by side reading the Sunday Star Tribune; folded the laundry and brought it home.

It was a nice little outing, actually.

But actually, it had been Bob who had balked at the buying of a washer and a dryer; Bob who had seen it as a needless expense, considering the Laundromat was only four blocks away and that it was a nice clean Laundromat and that they had come to know the owners so well and it was so reasonable to do the entire week's laundry.

But Bob was gone.

Bob was dead.

I don't want to be pushy, Lou...

But Kathleen had pushed and the next thing they knew, there they were in the washer and dryer section of Mister Demers' appliance store over on Penn, a few blocks from Lou's house, and Kathleen was grilling the owner about warranties and Lou was opening and shutting lids and perusing operating manuals and yanking out lint screens and generally having a time of it. It came down to a choice between a basic set and a one-step-up set, with Kathleen leaning toward basic. Lou surprised everyone, especially Mister Demers, by opting for the more expensive set.

If you're spending hundreds of dollars, what's another dollar or two? Besides, I like the do-dads on this one. Lou tapped a fingernail on the surface of the one-step-up washer. And that was that and that was how the washer and dryer came to be sitting in Lou's basement, draped with old sheets and looking – once Benjamin removed the sheets – pretty much as they had looked twenty years earlier in Mister Demers' store up the street.

Kathleen didn't have to ask what Lou thought about when she went downstairs to do her laundry.

I can't imagine how I got along without them all those years. Goodness.

Three days after they'd bought the appliances, Kathleen took Lou out to look for a new television set.

Isn't this sinful?

No, they told her. It's what people do, Lou. They spend their money on things that will make them happy, or more comfortable, or both. You can't take it with you. As Bob had discovered.

And as Lou had discovered when they took her to the Trust Company, Bob had left quite a lot of it behind.

A few weeks after Kathleen and Benjamin had returned home, Lou called: they'd never recognize the place. She'd had a man come in to paint and paper the whole main floor. As soon as the paint was dry, she had a company come in and replace all the broadloom. As soon as the carpeting was down, she had another company come in and take away the sofas and chairs and recover them.

It's like a brand new house. Bob wouldn't recognize the place.

He'd have had a hard time recognizing his wife, too.

Lou had become a new woman. One with a bank account and a cheque book. She was like a kid who stops just inside the door of the chocolate shop, savouring the smells, who turns to ask her parents if she can have something, only to realize her parents are no-where in sight.

Lou confessed to feeling a little guilty. For the first few moments after buying the washer and dryer she could almost hear Bob tsk-tsk-ing in the background. But she had never put much stock in guilt – too Catholic – and figured she was too old to start.

And it wasn't as though she was going to run out of money any time soon. Or in her lifetime. Which she'd discovered, much to her surprise, when the Trust Company man had explained to Lou the nature of her situation.

In a nutshell her situation was this: he says I don't have to count my nickels, or my dimes. Or my dollars, for that matter.

She thought they should drink to that.

And they had.

You must be Benjamin.

Hm?

Benjamin stood, smiled, offered his hand (though it was impolite, he seemed to recall, for a gentleman to offer his hand to a lady; should wait until she offered hers, then grip it firmly but gently, never squeeze: the legacy of Luther Miles).

The woman, mid-fifties, short, thin with a nun-like smile and demeanor, accepted his hand and shook it, firmly. I'm Dorothy Fullum, Lucille's social worker.

Dorothy Fullum smiled past Benjamin and leaned over Lou's bed. Hi Lou.

Lou stirred, opened her eyes a sliver, then shut them again. Said nothing.

How are you today?

No response.

Isn't it nice that Benjamin has come to visit? You must be pleased.

Lou opened her eyes again, a little wider this time. Yes, she said. I am. She smiled at Benjamin then shut her eyes once more.

Do you want to sleep?

Yes.

Then you don't mind if I steal Benjamin for a few moments?

Where are you going?

I thought I'd take him downstairs for a coffee, something to eat. He must be getting hungry. It's just about lunch time.

Lunch time?

Benjamin glanced at his watch.

Eleven thirty-three.

Time flies.

That would be nice, said Lou.

We'll see you in a few moments.

I should still be here.

Dorothy laughed, then nodded in the direction of the door and Benjamin followed her around the nursing station and down the corridor and – Dorothy punching the escape code – down the back stairway to the basement and the staff cafeteria. Not very elegant, said Dorothy, but they make good sandwiches and the soup is generally excellent, if you're in the mood for soup.

For the next twenty minutes – while Benjamin ate his barley soup and sliced chicken sandwich – Dorothy brought him up to speed on the deterioration of Lou's condition, dates and details, over the past several weeks; outlined the options suggested by the nurses and doctors who had been caring for her, the options which remained.

The nursing staff had convened a plan-of-care meeting at which all the professionals who had been involved with Lou over the past few weeks were invited to make comments and suggestions about her care and treatment. I asked Lou to come, but she refused. She said she couldn't see how it could take an entire committee to decide what should happen to one little ninety-two year old woman. And besides, she really didn't think it was anyone's business. She'd already convened her own plan-of-care meeting and decided she wanted to die. She said it was a unanimous decision. Dorothy tipped her head a little to the left and smiled. And shook her head. There really aren't that many options. She is ninety-two. She's lucid. She wants to die. If there was dementia and she was refusing to eat, we could order a feeding regimen. But really, she seems to be very clear, very sharp.

And very determined, said Benjamin.

Exactly, said Dorothy. I would have some very serious reservations about ordering forced feeding. I think we all would. We talked about it, quite a lot. But in the end we wondered whether we wouldn't simply be imposing our will on Lucille and we decided we would be and we didn't think that in this case we had the right to do that. That's why we were all anxious to have you get here. We really needed someone in the family to give us direction.

I'm not exactly family, said Benjamin.

As far as Lou is concerned, you're family. The only family she's got. And if you're family as far as she's concerned, you're family as far as we're concerned. Dorothy turned her mug by its handle. Has she talked much today?

Not much. Except to say she wants to die.

She's told me the same thing any number of times. She said she wanted to go see your Uncle Bob. And she wants to see her Mother.

She says she has some questions she wants answered.

Benjamin knew the questions.

At least some of them.

When Benjamin came down in May to help Lou sort through the remnants of her life, clean out the drawers, empty the filing cabinets, fill boxes to be taken to The Home, fill boxes to be taken to the trash, she had turned in her chair in front of her desk: did I ever tell you about my Mother?

Lou was nine years old when her Mother died. Cruel loss: Lou's Father dead just six years earlier. She could remember him, but barely. He had been a tall man, and robust – the photographs revealed as much – and he had been a gentle man and greatly devoted to his children, but to Lou most especially.

He had fallen ill with tuberculosis and though he rallied for a time, the illness gradually suffocated him.

His death had stunned Lou's Mother. Though she had known her husband was ill, she had never allowed herself to think he might die. And when he did, she was left alone with four children, had no money, had to go back to New York and clean other people's houses in order to pay the rent, make ends meet. It had become harder and harder to do that.

Her Mother had never been a strong woman, physically. She was of average height but never carried an extra pound on her fragile frame. She was a striking woman, as Benjamin could tell at a glance from the photographs Lou had framed and hung over her desk. A little austere, she seemed, though that might just have been a pose for the photographer.

If life had been fair – and when in the history of the world has it ever been? – Lou's Mother would have married a wealthy man and been kept in fitting style: living in a large home with one or two maids; spending her days reading or playing the piano. She had been a voracious reader, as a child, and a talented musician. She had been courted by a young man who might have opened the door to just such a life – a young physician, just starting out, a man who had joined her family's church. Lou's Grandmother had favoured the match, invited the young doctor for Sunday supper a number of times. But Lou's

Mother had followed her heart, rather than her head, or her Mother's advice.

She ran off with a carpenter, a hauntingly good-looking man: gentle, thoughtful and kind.

And he had died.

And then Lou's Mother had died and upon her death, the children were separated: Harry out on his own, Norman and David and Lou packed off separately to live with aunts and uncles.

Lou was sent to Toms Creek, a little mining town in the Virginia mountains, to live with Mother's brother Donald and his wife and his six children.

You will find Toms Creek on a map, or in memory.

On the map, it is a small black dot in southwestern Virginia, a couple of miles north of Coeburn. It is at the end of a long valley shouldered on the one side by the Blue Ridge Mountains and on the other by the Appalachians.

In Lou's memory, Toms Creek is a huddle of wood-frame buildings – houses and store, stables and school house, hospital and post office – in a cove of green.

Green was the colour of those years in the valleys of Virginia. In those days – as today – wild vines grew over everything that did not move. Kudzu, they called it.

You lie there reading that book all day, said Aunt Willa, and the vines will grow right over you. We'll never be able to find you.

Uncle's house was at the edge of Toms Creek, its front door facing the crushed-coal roadway, its rear door opening onto a verandah that looked over a field which undulated down to the creek known as Toms Gist which ran along the base of the mountains, the Appalachians. There were trees by the creek and the vines – a sort of wild grape – had grown right over one of those trees. It looked, from a distance, as though the tree was wearing a dress, green velvet. Separate those vines, crawl between them, and you found yourself in a kind of natural tent – cool whatever the heat of the day. You could look out between the vines and see everything that was going on in the yard but no-one – even if only a few feet distant – could see you sitting in your secret hiding place.

The Hiding Tree became Lou's favourite place. She would sit by the hour, knees drawn to chest, arms around her shins, sit and watch her cousins in the yard, her aunt on the verandah, her uncle in the field. It was like watching a film. All those people so close, but not quite real.

Lou often imagined her own family sitting with her under The Hiding Tree: organized elaborate tea parties for them with cookies and cakes. She could almost feel them, so real were they. Could almost hear them: laughter and chatter.

And the Hiding Tree became her Reading Tree as well. It was there she came to meet the Bronte Sisters; read their sorrowful tales of love sought and lost. It was there she sat and read, sat and dreamt. And her dreams, of course, were always of home.

Her first and lasting impression – stepping from the train – was the sound of the coal rattling down the conveyor into the waiting railway cars; a sound that never ceased, even on Christmas Day.

Uncle Donald and Aunt Willa lived in a two-storey house at the edge of the town. It needed more than paint.

Aunt Willa was initially welcoming. But six months on, she had become resentful.

I don't blame her, Lou had said in one of several retellings of the story of her childhood. They had a hard enough time feeding their own children, never mind the child of a dead sister. At the time, though, Lou did not regard her aunt in such a charitable light. I hated her. And she matched her aunt, resentment for resentment and this had sparked resentment, in turn, in Lou's cousins and these resentments had broken out in the heat and smoke of daily battles, battles which Lou was doomed to lose and from which she had no place to turn for solace or help. It was like living in a bad novel, she had once told Benjamin. Or having a starring role in a B movie –Joan Crawford on one of her bad days. I could hardly wait to get out of there.

But wait she had had to do: for seven seemingly endless years of bickering and snickering and, ultimately, silence. When I was sixteen, I left, went to New York. Got a job. I was never so grateful to get out of any place in my life. She never saw any of them – aunt, uncle or cousins – again. Nor did she see any of her brothers ever again.

Norman, she knew, had died. And she supposed Harry and David had died as well, though she never did hear from or of them again. For many years, certainly those first few after Benjamin had come back into her life, she held out the hope that Harry or David would some day miraculously show up on her doorstep, call her on the telephone.

Impossible, of course.

She presumed Harry would be dead by then. He was half a dozen years older than she.

But little David: it plagued her at nights to think that he might still be out there somewhere, wondering what had happened to his sister, wondering where she might be, wondering whether she ever thought of him as he thought of her.

He would have had no way of tracking her, even if he'd wanted to. She'd married a man he'd never heard of and moved so long ago from New York there could be no way for him ever to pick up her very faint trail.

For all she knew, he might be living right here in Minneapolis. Maybe a few blocks away, or on the other side of town. Or maybe down the road in Iowa or over in Wisconsin. On a farm, perhaps. David had always loved farms, professed the desire when he was a little boy to grow up and buy his own farm: chickens and cows and corn so high you'd get lost in the rows.

You heard such stories, from time to time, read them in the newspaper: brothers and sisters, mothers and daughters, fathers and sons reunited after years of searching for each other when all those years their paths had been crossing and re-crossing and they could not imagine how, during all those years – they must have seen each other who knows how many times – they did not actually recognize each other.

Lou was certain she'd have recognized David. His face might have changed. But his eyes couldn't change. Mother's eyes.

But she never got the chance.

There was no happily-ever-after for Lou and her brothers.

It was all a fantasy.

Just wishful thinking.

The fact was, she and David would never meet again in this life.

In this life, Lou was alone in the world.

Except for you two, and the children. Lou patted Benjamin, then Kathleen, on the knee. Smiled at them and shook her head.

I always thought: if only Mother hadn't died. Everything might have turned out so much better.

But Mother had died.

And when Benjamin asked how she had died, the answer was always the same: She died of a broken heart.

What do you think?

Hm?

Benjamin looked up from his coffee, cooling in its mug. Think?

About our options? said Dorothy

Benjamin pushed his mug aside. What are our options?

We could order forced feeding, if you really wanted to try that. For a time. Or we could just authorize comfort care.

Which means?

Nothing intrusive. Medication for pain, should she need it. The normal sanitary care. But that would be about it.

Just let her fade away?

Yes.

Hm.

You don't have to decide anything right this minute. But they'll need to know, sooner than later.

Have you talked to Lou about this?

No.

I'd like to.

Of course.

And we'll have to decide what to do with her things. If she's not going back to her apartment, we should think of sorting through her possessions. We can put some of her things in storage, until you come back to pick them up. And if you wish, we can donate the rest to missions for the needy. Maybe later this afternoon you could go to her apartment and have a look through her things.

Sure, said Benjamin. I can do that.

Someone had shut the lights in Lou's room. Shut the lights and turned on a fan on the far side of the privacy curtain, where the radio played on.

Twelve eighteen.

Lou was still sleeping.

Lou?

No response.

Lou was on a train. They were rolling down the valley in Virginia – the Blue Ridge Mountains hazy and distant in the east, the Appalachians nearer and greener in the west.

Lou had slept through much of Pennsylvania, but she was awake now, awake and alert, had a curious sense of excitement and forboding as the train carried her further and further into the southland and, with every mile, further from all she knew of the world, all that was dear and familiar.

She wondered, looking up at the mountains – a world of green to her right – what Harry and Norman and David might be looking at as they, too, made their unfamiliar journey into their futures. She wondered whether they would ever see each other again.

The train slowed and then stopped and the conductor who had led her to her seat in New York now stood above her.

This is your stop, Miss.

He brought her suitcase – Mother's suitcase, blue with black edging and a black handle – down from the rack above her head.

This way, Miss.

She followed him down the car and into the space at the end where the half door was open.

She smelled Virginia for the first time; the air humid and heavy with pines and flowers. Like a hothouse, she thought.

The conductor opened the door and descended the stair, setting her suitcase upon the wood-plank platform. He reached up to take her hand. Mind your step, Miss.

She took his hand. It was a huge hand, and warm. Unusually soft, she thought, for a man's hand.

And there she was, feet on the ground of her new home.

Toms Creek. Just about as far south as you can be, and still be in Virginia, said the Conductor. Is someone to meet you?

Yes, she said. My Uncle.

The Conductor looked down the platform at the people who had come to meet the train.

Do you see him?

I don't know him, she said. I've never met him.

Oh, said the Conductor. What's his name?

Donald, she said. Donald Sutter.

You wait here, he said. I'll be right back. And off he went, toward the clutch of people at the far end of the platform.

Donald Sutter? Is there a Donald Sutter here?

There was no Donald Sutter among the farmers and the miners on the platform.

Does anyone know Mister Sutter?

I do, said a woman. He lives not far from here. Just out at the edge of town.

Would this woman be good enough to look after the little girl down at the other end of the platform until her Uncle came to fetch her?

The woman said she would be happy to wait with the child until Donald Sutter showed, if he did remember to show up – I swear that man will be late for his own funeral – and followed the Conductor back down the platform to where Lou was standing, beside her suitcase.

Lou thanked the Conductor who wished her luck and happiness and watched him climb the stairs, and shut the half door, then lean out and wave toward the engineer and the train began chugging down the line and around the bend and out of sight.

You've come to stay? said the woman.

Yes, said Lou.

Oh, said the woman.

Mother died, said Lou. And Father before her. So we're being taken in by relatives.

We?

My brothers and me.

The woman looked down the platform.

They're not here, said Lou. They've gone off to live with other relatives. I'm the only one who's come here to live with Uncle Donald.

Well, said the woman, look who's decided to make an appearance.

Uncle Donald drove his team and wagon up the road and across the graveled yard and pulled to a stop not far from where Lou and the woman stood.

Why thank you, Shirley. Kind of you, to be sure. I lost track of time, it seems.

Donald Sutter looked down at his niece, looped the reins around the bar across the front of his wagon and stepped down. He looked her up and down and extended his hand. I'm your Uncle Donald.

She shook his hand – large and rough, coal dust embedded beneath his nails. He was a tall man, much taller than Mother, and broad across the shoulders. His hair was curly, where Mother's was straight. But when he smiled, it was Mother's smile.

Pleased to meet you, sir.

Likewise, he said. He looked at her for a long moment: you are the image of her, right enough. Right down to the hair. He shook his head, as though shuddering.

Lou didn't know what to do, so she said merely: thank you, sir. Then picked up her suitcase.

I'll take that for you. Donald Sutter lifted the suitcase into the back of the wagon, then lifted Lou up and into the front.

Ever been in a horse-drawn wagon, Lucille?

No, she said.

Well, you can't have driven one then, can you?

No sir.

Would you like to?

Drive? she said.

Yes, he said.

Yes, she said.

He showed her how to hold the reins, looping them loosely around either wrist. Say git and they'll go.

Git, she said.

And so it was that the little girl with the auburn hair – the image of her Mother – drove herself away from all that was familiar, out of her past and into her future, a stranger at her side.

Where were you?

Hm? Oh. Hi. I didn't realize you were awake. I must have been dozing myself.

Where did you two go?

Down the basement, to the cafeteria.

What were you talking about?

You.

And what were you saying?

We were talking about what to do for you.

Do for me?

In terms of care.

I'm getting all the care I need, or want.

Do you want things to just go the way they're going?

Going?

You don't want the nurses to try to get you to eat?

I'd eat if I wanted to. Which I don't. I just want them to leave me alone. I'd like you to tell them that.

I will if you wish.

I do.

All right. I'll do that.

Can you get me some water?

Benjamin held the cup close to her lips, positioning the straw. Lou drank, then released the straw. That's enough. And then: Thank you.

Do you want anything else?

No.

Can I ask you something?

Silence.

Why are you doing this, Lou?

Doing what?

Starving yourself.

I don't want to live.

Why not?

Look around, Benjamin. I can't live here any longer.

I don't want you to die, Lou.

We all die, Benjamin. Sooner or later. And now it's my turn. It's not such a big affair, really. She patted his hand and smiled. Really.

Hello, Lucille. How are you doing? The nurse stopped at the end of the bed, reached down and touched Lou's foot. No response.

The nurse looked at Benjamin and smiled.

Benjamin shrugged.

Could you wait out in the hall for a few minutes? I just want to check her. Make sure she's dry.

Dry? he thought

Benjamin looked at the nurse, then at Lou. Sure, he said, no problem.

He hadn't thought of Lou in diapers. Hadn't thought of any of these others in diapers, either, although they all must be wearing them, incapable as they were of going to the washroom when need be. And how would that feel? Hm? Having strange hands struggle plastic diapers under your butt and up between your thighs, strange hands fiddling with sticky-tabs, cinching the top of the diapers tight to your gut so there'd be no leaks?

Out in the common room, the diapered oldsters were parked just where they'd been parked the last time he'd walked past: all of them staring intently at the television, some kind of soap opera now.

Benjamin skirted them and walked down the hall toward the elevators. On either side of the hall there were rooms where patients were allowed to have some of their own furniture. They were down to the essentials now: a chair, a table, a television, a hospital bed, a school-style locker with a few articles of clothing.

The constriction of lives, people spinning off the stuff they'd spent their entire lives accumulating. Some kind of centrifugal force kicking in. Benjamin could see all that stuff – computers, books, paintings, dishes, glasses, knick-knacks flying off into space, people ducking to get out of the way as the detritus of another life went flying past.

Getting and spending... Wordsworth smilingly intoned... we lay waste our powers. Yes, Bill.

True enough. But in the end, the laugh's on us, isn't it? All those things we'd fought so hard to get and to keep, just so much forgotten junk now. As his own Mother once said: we never really own anything. We're just custodians. All the stuff we guard so jealously, all of it will end up in someone else's hands some day. Someone else's hands, or the junkyard. It would do, she thought, not to spend too much of your time buying and acquiring and stockpiling.

All along the wall, residents sat in their wheelchairs. There were nine of them, one in front of the other, all facing the same direction. They looked like they were on a bus, going nowhere.

Benjamin walked to the far end of the hall, then turned and walked slowly back the way he'd come, had to walk the gauntlet of stares.

Save for one, the old people in the wheelchairs didn't seem to see him. But that one – an ancient slumping man – managed a gummy smile.

When Benjamin got back to the common room, the curtain was still drawn around Lou's bed. He stood to the side of the nursing station, wondering what to do with himself.

Excuse us, Benjamin.

Two nurses smiled past him, pushing a crane-like device. Want a ride? One of the nurses giggled.

The machine had a long arm, parallel to the floor, from which hung a canvas hammock which swung to and fro.

I'll walk, but thanks for the offer.

Well, if you change your mind, let us know.

They negotiated the crane through the doorway of Lou's room, then past Lou's curtained bed to the far end of the room. As they went by, the nurse pulled back the curtain around Lou's bed. She'd adjusted Lou's covers, then motioned for Benjamin to come back in.

She's fine. She's dry.

Benjamin thanked her.

Are you her son?

I'm her godson.

The one from Canada?

Benjamin nodded.

Well, Lucille, aren't you the lucky one? A visitor all the way from Canada. And a good-looking one at that.

Lou said nothing.

The nurse smiled and extended her hand. I'm Helen. Nice to meet you.

Benjamin shook her hand, though not without thinking of diapers. Nice to meet you too.

Lou, you should be talking with your godson. You'll have lots of time to sleep later on, once he's gone.

Yes, Benjamin thought. That she would.

Silence.

Time for a change of scenery, Dolores.

Dolores gurgled, then coughed, then gurgled some more.

It was like a shadow-show on the curtain which separated Lou's half of the room from Dolores' half. Benjamin watched the silhouettes as the nurses spent a few moments working the canvas hammock under Dolores.

Is she straight?

She looks straight.

Then there was a whining sound as the machine winched the old lady up out of her bed. The nurses turned the crane and lowered Dolores into an easy chair, then slid the hammock out from under her and adjusted her so that she was sitting upright, more or less. One of the nurses rolled the crane out of the room. The other followed, pushing Dolores along in her armchair on wheels.

Dolores didn't seem to notice, staring at the ceiling, mouth agape as if she was about to say something, if only she could remember what it was she had wanted to say.

Nothing like a change of surroundings, said Helen, as Dolores went silently past. Helen turned and smiled at Benjamin and shrugged her eyebrows. Then she, too, left the room.

The nurse parked Dolores near the television.

Dolores didn't seem to notice.

What was all the commotion?

The nurses were just moving Dolores out into the common room so she can watch television. Would you like to watch television?

No.

Would you like to get into your wheelchair? I could drive you around the ward for a while. Or we could go downstairs to the lounge.

No, said Lou. I just want to sleep.

Lou had turned to face him, but her eyes were closed.

Lou?

Yes.

You didn't answer my question.

Which question?

I asked you why you wanted to die.

I can't live here anymore.

In this room?

Yes.

If you ate something, got your strength back, you could move back into your apartment.

I can't live here any more, Benjamin.

Why?

Look around, Benjamin. Lou sighed, then turned. I hope God hasn't forgotten me.

A few moments later, Benjamin checked the clock.

Twelve fifty-three.

Lou was snoring.

Asleep and dreaming.

Lou was in the kitchen of her Aunt's house in Virginia.

Don't just stand there, Lou. Lend a hand. Aunt Willa pushed a strand of hair from her forehead with the back of her wrist. She had dark hair, almost black, which she cut short, like a man's. She was a short woman – she came only to Uncle Donald's shoulder – and thin. The only thing large about her was her impatience. She seemed always to be scowling. Scowling and angry. Angry and exasperated.

What would you have me do?

Do? Have a look about you child. There's lots to do. Dishes. Dusting. Cleaning the floor.

Lou chose the dishes: took the kettle from the top of the wood-stove where it always sat simmering, carried it to the sink. She put the stopper in the sink then poured the water from the kettle. She added some cold water from the bucket on the counter until the water was no longer scalding.

Her aunt – busy at the stove – looked at what Lou was doing and crossed the room, put her own finger in the water in the sink.

Dishes will never get clean in luke-warm water, Lou. I've told you that before.

But...

Never mind the excuses. Go fill the kettle and the bucket, we'll heat some more.

Lou carried the kettle and the bucket to the back yard and pumped them full from the well. She carried them back inside, one at a time.

You're always making work for yourself, Lou. Carry them in at the same time and you've saved yourself twenty steps. When you're old and creaky and your legs are giving out, you'll wish you had.

Lou couldn't imagine old and creaky.

She couldn't imagine sixteen – the age when she could leave this place and go back to Brooklyn – never mind sixty-six.

She put the kettle on to boil.

Don't just stand there, Lou. Idle hands are the Devil's workshop. Take a broom to the floor while you're waiting for the water to boil.

Make yourself useful.

Lou had never had to make herself useful in Brooklyn. In Brooklyn, she had simply to be.

But everything had changed the day Mother left the flat and failed to return.

Everything had changed and Lou knew that no matter how long she lived, how old and creaky she might get, things would never again be the way they had been when she and Mother and the boys were living together in that walkup in Brooklyn.

The floor won't sweep itself, Lou. You have to move the broom, dear. Honestly, I don't know…

Aunt Willa sighed an exasperated sigh. You'll be the death of me, Lou, I swear.

She was about to say something else but said instead: I'm sorry, Lou. I shouldn't have said that.

Lou swept the floor and when the floor was swept – the dustpan emptied in the yard – the kettle was whistling and Lou went at the dishes, her hands red and stinging in the scalding water.

That's better, her aunt said, testing the water.

Lou could hear her cousins out in the yard, laughing and chattering. She did not wish to be out there with them – they rarely made her feel welcome – but she wished they would choose some other place to play, a place out of earshot, back of the barn or out in the fields, or up in the schoolyard.

Wished they would go elsewhere, or that Aunt Willa would send her on an errand.

Go get some bread, Lou.

Lou loved to go on errands, loved those moments of being alone, alone with her thoughts.

Down the road – beyond Mister Stilwell's stables and the machine shop and the supply house – was Hunk Town, that part of Toms Creek where the Hungarian miners and their families lived. As soon as you passed the supply house you could smell the bread baking in the brick oven in Mrs. Kisfaludy's yard. Lou would give Mrs. Kisfaludy a nickel – which the portly woman dropped into the pocket of her apron – and held out a teatowel in both hands and Mrs. Kisfaludy would open the door of the oven and remove a loaf of bread on a wooden paddle and place it on the teatowel and Lou would wrap the towel around the loaf and cradle the swaddled loaf the way you would cradle a baby, feeling its warmth against her arms and her chest all the way home.

Go get some eggs, Lou.

The eggs, and everything else, were to be found at the company store. It was a huge store – or seemed so to Lou at the time – where you could buy meat or clothes or groceries or furniture or a casket – one standing in the rear corner of the store as though to serve as some kind of reminder to those who came in. Lou remembers daydreaming her way through the furniture department – running her fingers over the waxed and polished surface of the dining room sets and the bedroom sets, dreaming of a time when she would buy just such a set for the flat she would one day rent in Brooklyn.

Go get the mail, Lou.

And Lou would pull open the door of the post office – setting the bells to ringing, bells on a leather strap hanging from an L-shaped strip of metal nailed to the frame above the door – and Mister Tompkins the postmaster would go to the wall behind the counter – a wall of cubbyhole mailslots – and fetch out letters and bills wrapped in a rubber band and slide them across the counter.

Lou would always leaf through these letters looking at the names on the envelopes and would always say: is there anything else for us, Mister Tompkins?

And every once in a great while, Mister Tompkins would go back to the wall and make a great show of looking in Uncle Donald's mail slot and turn and shake his head and then – faint smile – oh, wait a minute, Lou. And would reach under the counter and produce an envelope across which Harry had written:

Miss Lucille Sutter

Toms Creek Virginia.

Oh.

Oh, thank you Mister Tompkins. Thank you very much.

Not at all, Miss Lucille. Not at all.

And Lou would run all the way from the post office and hand Aunt Willa her bundle of mail and then run out of the house and into the field behind the barn, across the field and burrow into her hiding spot beneath the pin oak tree. And would squat on the cool earth, knees against her chest, and would look at the handwriting on the front of the envelope, look at the carefully printed letters and see Harry's hand as he held the pen to the paper, could see Harry's hand and arm and smiling face; watched him finish writing her name, licking and sealing the envelope and then, carefully, ever so carefully, she would pull the flap of the envelope and open it, trying not to tear the paper, and would pull out his letter.

Dear Lou...

Pull out his letter... I am living now in... and the dollar bill he always enclosed.

... a dollar for a treat, Lou...

... do you still like peppermints?...

... think of me when you are eating your candy, Lou...

And when she had read the letter and re-read it – committing it, finally, to memory – she would fold it and return it to the envelope and, just as Harry had done, would run the tip of her tongue along the glued edge of the flap, lick it and seal it, tuck it in the top of her dress.

Run to the store.

Peppermints? And Mister Becker, in his apron behind the counter, would say – let's see, I'm sure we have some peppermints here somewhere.

And then, paper bag in her hand, Lou would run back through the village and across the field to her hiding tree and there, in the cool green, would open the bag and take out one of the mints and put it on the end of her tongue, savouring its taste, before taking it into her mouth. And would sit there, thinking of Harry, thinking of Harry and Norman and David, thinking of the boys and wondering what they were doing, what they were thinking about at that exact moment, wondered if they were thinking of her as she was thinking of them, would think of them until the last of the peppermint had dissolved in her mouth.

Would run home – bag of mints in her hand, Harry's letter against the skin of her chest, young heart singing.

She would run up the stairs and squirrel the bag of mints away under the mattress, would allow herself one mint a day, then one every other day, then one every three days, hoping another letter would arrive before the mints ran out.

Faint hope.

Where have you been, Lou?

I've been calling you and calling you.

I've been out in the fields.

Lou loved the fields around her aunt and uncle's home. The fields and the trees and the hills beyond. When her aunt allowed her the time, Lou would slip around the end of the barn and walk across the fields and into the woods. Sometimes she found a place to her liking and sat down in the sun, feeling the warmth, feeling the wind, listening to the birds and the rustling of the leaves and the pines. Sometimes, though, she went directly into the woods and walked until, turning around, she could no longer see the house or the barn though she could still hear – you could always hear – the coal scuttling down the chute and clattering into the waiting rail cars.

She wondered, walking in the woods, how long it would take to walk clear through the woods and over the hills to the highway and how long it would take to walk down that highway all the way back to Brooklyn. But when she thought of this, she wondered what she would do if she did get back to Brooklyn; the boys scattered, the flat let out to strangers. She wondered if ever again she would feel at home anywhere in the world the way she had felt at home in that place.

But she did not often think of this, for it made her sad.

When she was sad, Aunt Willa would scold her: put away that long face, Lou. You've got your sorrows, Lord knows, but we all have our sorrows and we must overcome them. Count your blessings, child, starting with the fact that you woke up this morning.

Lou wondered about her Aunt's sorrows, wondered what they could be. She had a home and a family. What sorrows could you have if you had all that? If Lou ever had a home and a family she was certain she would never feel sorrowful again. But she wasn't sure she would ever have either home or family again. That was in the future. And the future seemed a very long way from Viriginia: time and space.

Sometimes, sitting in the field or walking through the woods or lying in bed at night, awake when all the others were sleeping, Lou found herself wondering about the future.

She wondered if she would ever see the boys again – though Harry promised to find work and get a place where they could all live. She didn't want to doubt him, but a year had passed already and he still didn't have a place. He would write as soon as he did. He promised. But the days unfolded into weeks and the weeks into months and Lou was still in Virginia.

And Lou had to press down the awful feeling that none of that would ever happen.

If it didn't happen, if they all grew up and went out into the world alone, Lou wondered what that world would be like.

One thing was certain: she would go back to Brooklyn. She would find a job and rent a flat of her own, even if she couldn't be with the boys.

Beyond that, she couldn't imagine.

She didn't want to live by herself, but she had no idea how this solitary life might end. She could imagine children – a house full of children – but she couldn't imagine a husband.

She couldn't imagine how she would find one.

How did people go about finding husbands and wives?

She asked her Aunt, but Aunt Willa just laughed and said: you're a little young to be looking for a husband, Lou.

But if you want to get one, you'd better learn how to keep a house. Keep a house, keep a man. Go strip the beds and wash the sheets. Your husband is going to want clean sheets, and he'll want…

Want what? Lou had wondered.

Never mind, Lou. Get up the stairs and at those beds. Your husband will wait.

There had been a smile in her Aunt's voice.

And that smile in her Aunt's voice made Lou feel even smaller than she already felt.

And that was one of the feelings she would always associate with her years in Virginia.

She never imagined seven years could feel like such an eternity.

And she was never so happy as when – duffle bag on her lap – her

Uncle Donald drove her by team and wagon to the train station and said: goodbye Lou. Good luck.

Four words.

And then – git – he slapped the reins and was driving away, back to the farm and Lou had stood there on the platform, sixteen years old, staring her future in the eye.

Ten minutes later – three minutes past one – Benjamin was parking the rental car by the side of the road which circled Lake Harriet. There are dozens of lakes in Minneapolis – Benjamin thought it one of the loveliest cities he'd seen – and this little lake a couple of miles from Lou's home was one of his favourites. He locked the car, pocketed the keys, crossed the road and sat on a bench, facing the water.

Their bench: his and Lou's.

Every summer, the past twenty summers, he and Lou had driven to the lake; sat and watched the sun play on the water, the clouds drift past in the blue beyond; listened to the children, listened to the birds; listened to their thoughts, listened to each other.

Their last visit, this past summer, they'd idled around the lake, just more than a mile; passed the botanical gardens and the concert shell, the ice-cream shop near which the sailboats were moored to their buoys in the bay. Then they'd circled the lake a second time so Lou could see it all from a different perspective, shadows and sunlight, and make up her mind: butterscotch or chocolate mint.

Then they drove around the lake again, parked in their usual spot, crossed the road to their bench beside the walking trail beside the shore – Lou holding onto her cone with one hand and Benjamin's arm with her other; Benjamin holding up his ice-cream cone, traffic-cop style, to stop oncoming cars as he and Lou turtled across the road.

This is perfect, Lou had thought.

And despite the fact Lou's feet didn't quite touch the earth when she had adjusted herself comfortably on the bench – had she shrunk? or had she always been this small? – it really was a perfect place to spend an hour of a summer afternoon. For quite some time after settling on the bench they didn't talk much: remarking on a sailboat lazing along the far shore, the beauty – or otherwise – of the dogs which trotted along beside their owners, tongues damply lolling.

It was one of these dogs – a chocolate Lab named Abby – that had got Lou going on the subject of dogs. As soon as the owner unhooked its leash, the Lab bounded over the low retaining wall and made a dash across the beach to the lake, landing with a splash in front of Benjamin and Lou.

Lou loved Labs. She and Robert had one – this was a long time ago – two or three years after they were married. They'd moved from Manhattan to a farmhouse out in Jersey. It seemed like something out of a storybook at first. They'd rented the house and bought Chester. They stayed in the country a little less than a year. Robert loved it at first but had come – especially that first winter – to hate commuting. So they moved back to Manhattan the following summer. It had broken their hearts to have to leave the dog behind, but they had no choice. Chester was a country dog. He was accustomed to the run of the fields around the farmhouse. He would have hated life in the city, hated life in an apartment. Robert had been right about that. So they left Chester at the neighbouring farm and drove off. They couldn't look back once they'd started to drive away. And it took them quite a long while (two more moves, the second bringing them to Minneapolis) before Lou could bring herself to hang the framed black and white snapshot of Chester on the kitchen wall (a snapshot now hanging above the bureau in her little apartment at the Home). Having that dog, Lou thought, was like having a baby – almost – Labs being so bright and curious and affectionate. When Robert got up and went from one room to the next, Chester got up and followed. When Lou went out to the yard to do a bit of gardening, Chester flopped on the grass nearby. When Lou and Robert sat on the loveseat in the evening, reading their books, listening to their records, Chester positioned himself so that he could touch both of them: chin on one foot, a paw on another. It sounded hopelessly sentimental to say so, Lou said with an embarrassed smile, but that dog – within days of their bringing him home – was the light of their lives.

Robert used to joke that I was getting to love the dog more than I loved him.

Lou wondered whether, when she got to Heaven – assuming she would get to Heaven – Chester would be waiting with all the others to welcome her. She turned to Benjamin: do you think dogs get to go to Heaven?

That hadn't been something Benjamin had spent much time thinking about. Taking another lick of his cone, he asked for a moment to consider it. During that moment, Abby the Lab, who had started all this speculation, bounded out of the lake, came dripping across the grass and – standing directly in front of Lou and Benjamin – gave himself a good and thorough shaking, splattering them both. The owner was profusely apologetic, but by this time Lou was scratching the offender under the chin, then feeding him the pointy remainder of her cone, then giving him a pat on his water-beaded head. The owner apologized once again. Lou told him not to concern himself, then told him about Chester, told him how much she loved Labs generally and Chester specifically, then she scratched the water-dog again and bid the owner and Abby good afternoon and she and Benjamin watched as they made their way down the path and out of sight around the bend.

Well?

Well, what?

The question of dogs and Heaven.

Give me a minute, said Benjamin.

A minute later: if Heaven was merely a more perfect rendering of life here on Earth, then obviously it would have to be equipped with dogs, bars and golf courses. If, however, Heaven was a reward for those faithful servants who had clung doggedly to their beliefs and to the straight and narrow path, shunning sin, doing good works, leaving the world a better place than they had found it (or, at the very least, no worse than they had found it) then clearly dogs – incapable of moral manoeuvring – couldn't make the cut.

Lou leapt to Chester's defence: if Heaven was a reward for those who made it through the strait gate, then clearly Chester would be there, wagging his tail, waiting for her. What kind of Heaven – and reward – would it be if the faithful got there and found their most treasured companions – two legs, or four – weren't there as well?

Benjamin conceded the point. There would be dogs in Heaven. No cats, however.

Lou was with him there.

Winded by their adventures in theology, they sat in silence for another ten or fifteen minutes, listening to the birds, listening to the children at play on the beach, watching the boats and the sun glinting on the waves which lapped on the shore near where they sat – prompting him to think of that line in a Bruce Cockburn song.

> All the diamonds in this world
> That mean anything to me
> Are conjured up by wind and sunlight
> Sparkling on the sea.

Lovely, said Lou.

Yes, said Benjamin.

And they went back to their silences; watching the people and the pets walking and jogging along the path which ran between them and the shore.

Why do you think we live? said Lou.

Hm?

Why do you think we're given a life to live, here on earth?

Benjamin was embarrassed to say he'd never thought about it; had merely taken it for granted.

Lou had him scrambling now, wanted to know if he meant he was just cruising through life, more or less unconsciously.

Well, he wouldn't say that, exactly.

What else was he saying if he was saying he'd never bothered to take a few minutes to figure out why he was wandering around here on earth as a human being, rather than spending his days as a stump, say, or a stone?

Well, he said.

Don't obfuscate, said Lou.

Well, he said. Yes. I guess.

Shame on you, she said again, giving him a nudge in the ribs.

Well, Mrs. Professor, why are we here?

Lou was not overly enamoured of the Catholic view of things – a little too much hocus-pocus, Latin and incense for her – but she thought St. Ignatius put his gnarly finger on it when he said that it was all pretty simple: man was created to Praise God and serve Him and, in so doing, to save his own soul. She thought – Catholic or not – that sort of summed things up. Thought the long and the short of it was this: life on earth was a kind of test drive. You were plunked down here, in this garden of earthly delights and detours and left to wander down this path or that, dodging the Devil, seeking the light at the end of the tunnel. If you avoided the bright lights of temptation and focused on the bright light of redemption, then you get to go to Heaven.

A little Sunday-schoolish, Benjamin thought, and said.

Lou didn't think Saint Augustine overly Sunday-schoolish. Or any of the other great thinkers – from Kierkegaard to Thomas Merton – who thought themselves down the same path toward more or less the same conclusion. Which you would think – another nudge in the ribs – a Mister Bachelor of Philosophy ought to know.

Question, said Benjamin. What are you going to miss most, once you're dead?

Nothing, said Lou.

Nothing?

Not a thing.

In Lou's view, everything was going to be a whole lot better and purer and more beautiful and peaceful in the place she was going – the place she was hoping to go – than it ever could be in the place she was shortly to leave. She would be rejoined with those she loved: Mother and Father, the boys and Robert. And you, too, she said, turning to face Benjamin. Though I'm in no hurry to see you up there. You can take your time joining me. Eternity lasts quite some time, I'm told. I won't mind waiting a few years to see you again.

Benjamin thought it was gracious of her to say so.

And was reminded of Rilke:

It's very hard to be dead
    And you try
    To make up for lost time
Till slowly you start
    To get whiffs
    Of eternity

I like that, Lou said, with what could only be described as a little-girl smile. I may have to steal it.

Go right ahead, said Benjamin. I did. And speaking of eternity, he wondered what she was going to do with all that time on her hands.

She would think of something. I expect I'll find sufficient to keep me interested. Life in Heaven has to be at least as interesting as life here on earth.

And she wouldn't mind having a little sit-down with The Creator, for whom she had a couple of questions.

Such as?

None of your business.

You really believe all that, don't you?

All what?

Heaven and God. Angels and eternity. All of that.

Of course, said Lou. She turned a surprised and concerned look upon him. Don't you?

Benjamin wished. He envied Lou her faith and her hope and her confidence. But where Lou saw light, he saw only shadows; while her heart was full of faith, his head was full of doubt and confusion.

No, he finally said. I can't say I do.

Don't you feel the presence of God all around you?

I can't say I do, Lou.

Oh dear.

Oh dear, indeed. Benjamin couldn't have said it better or more succinctly himself. It was a pity. He could sense that, simply by listening to people like Lou talking about their relationship with God. They spoke of God the way they would speak of a kindly uncle, or a favourite Grandfather; someone they knew to be attentive to them and ever watchful over them. On the one hand, he thought it ridiculous and pathetic that people would whittle God down to size and turn him into some kind of sentimental Buddy. But at the same time, he envied their ability to do so, even if they were deluding themselves; envied the comfort they seemed to get out of it all. But try as he might – and he had tried, Lord knows; had gone to church, said his prayers, sung the hymns – he could never entirely put his heart into Nearer My God To Thee. He was always on the outside when it came to God. He'd read the books: in fact, spent a week one summer in the hills of Kentucky at Gethsemani, the monastery where Thomas Merton had found his way, and his peace. Spent that week reading Merton, thinking to find in the pages of The Seven Storey Mountain some direction, perhaps, for his own spiritual quest. He found in Merton a reference to the theologian Etienne Gilson, and Gilson's wonderful conception of God: He is the pure act of existing. Or, as Merton had added: God is Being Itself. And, back to Gilson: that God is beyond any images of

Him that we might conjure up, is in fact beyond conceptualizing, is just out there, as Lou said, all around us. Which was a felt thing.

Benjamin was able to understand what Lou and these others were talking about when they spoke so fervently. But understanding didn't help. What they were talking about was not a matter of the intellect at all, but a matter of faith. Or belief. Kierkegaard's Great Leap. Which was exactly what they'd taken: like kids in a park, running down the hill, soaring into flight and landing on the far side of the creek. But Benjamin was the kind of kid who – if he had taken that run, would have landed in the middle of the creek. But he never took the run. He wandered the creek-bank, looking for a bridge. He'd never found the bridge, and never would. There were no bridges. Not across that creek. And he'd been in his forties by the time he figured that out.

Benjamin and Lou sat for a long time that day this past summer, staring into their own distances at their own horizons, not saying a word.

Now, these months later, sitting alone where they had sat together, he wasn't so sure he'd been entirely honest.

He rose and began walking along the path bordering the lake.

There were two paths, actually: one for walkers and joggers, the other for cyclists and skaters. Benjamin kept to the path nearer the lake, the one for walkers.

The first few summers he'd come to Minneapolis, Benjamin had been in the habit of jogging. Early each morning, before Lou and Kathleen and the children had wakened, he drove to the lake, parked the car and took a slow run around the shore. Those first dawning hours were a magical time of day. He found himself now and then saying a little prayer of thankfulness for the beauty of the morning and the gift of experiencing it. But though he uttered the words, and meant them, he could not have explained, then or now, to whom he was addressing that little prayer. He had no picture of God – certainly not the flowing beard and flashing eyes of the storybooks – any more than he had any sense of God, except that in some way this was a fearsome more than a loving Being. Certainly not Lou's loving God. Lou's God was a comforting and a comfortable presence in her life, a presence she apparently felt around her all the time.

Which would be some kind of gift, he thought.

But it was not a gift that had been bestowed upon Benjamin Miles.

And he was not sure that what he experienced running around the lake those years ago was really God at all.

Maybe it was just a runner's high.

One thing was certain: the feeling he had while running around the lake, or the feeling he had walking in Ojibway Park back home, was not a feeling he could replicate in a church. Churches – all their rituals and dogmas – left him feeling claustrophobic. How did anyone think that the God which created Heaven and Earth, which was revealed in the great vaulting heavens over our heads, could be stuffed into an airless little box. Even a box with stained-glass windows. How could anyone be deluded enough to think that God would fit into their boxes or into their ideologies? How could anyone experience God in a place so cut off from the God's own world of beauty, in a place so musty and droning, so petty and political, was a mystery to Benjamin. How anyone would want to try to do that was beyond him.

Well, Lou had a more charitable view of churches.

Churches, she thought, were a place where the hopeful, the hope-filled, could gather together and express publicly their private faith. Yes, she thought, churches were political – petty and political – and the choirs were filled with people who couldn't sing and the pulpits were full of people who couldn't preach, and the choirmaster ran off with the choirboy. But despite all that, despite all these painfully and obviously human faults, churches were filled with people who, by and large, were doing their best. They were singing, as best they could – in tune or otherwise – the praises of their God.

Yes, said Benjamin. He could see her point.

All well and good.

But this, he thought as he slowly circled the lake, taking in the sun and the sky and the trees, the water and the unexpected warmth of this October day, this was cathedral enough for him.

And the only kind that mattered.

Lou was in church.

She sat alone in a pew near the rear of the Little Church Around the Corner in lower midtown Manhattan. It was November 1927, Lou's first winter back in the city and she had walked from her rooming house and taken the trolley downtown, then walked the rest of the way. Her face was pink and her fingers still a little numb from the cold. She had forgotten how cold it could be in the city in the winter, winds knifing down the streets between the towering office buildings.

It was Mother who had discovered the old church on 29th Street, between Fifth and Madison. She had been out on one of her Sunday-morning walks – in those early lonely days she often went out and walked for hours – when she turned for no apparent reason onto 29th and saw the lynch-gate leading to the garden beside the church. Just inside the gate there was a statue of Jesus, hand lifted in a blessing. Under the gate enclosing the statue were carved the words: Come Unto Me and I Will Give You Rest.

Mother had thought the blessing was meant for her, particularly. It seemed as though Christ had spoken to her.

Beside the statue there was a fountain and on the other side a lectern for a Bible. Mother hadn't realized it, but the lectern was for a Bible to be used in a short service for the dead. The coffins were brought in through the lynch-gate and a brief service held there, under Jesus' watchful eye, before the corpse was taken inside for the service. A kind of way-station.

Mother had sat that first afternoon on one of the benches not far from the statue of Jesus, had removed her shoes, lifted her face to the sun. In the distance, she could see the Empire State building. She thought it a wonder – and told the children she would take them there next Sunday so they could see for themselves – that such an oasis had been created in the very heart of one of the busiest and noisiest cities in the world. Though the sounds of the city must have been clearly audible in that garden, Mother could not recall hearing them; had the sensation she was far from the city, in every sense of the word.

After Father died and they returned to the city, Mother could not bring herself to return to familiar places; she had found a new flat and refused to go back to the church where they had all gone together in happier times. Although Harry thought it might be a comfort – to sit again where they had all sat together – Mother shook her head: too many ghosts, Harry.

She told them that sitting in the garden of The Little Church, and later in the church itself, she felt a sense of comfort. Hard to explain. Perhaps they would feel it themselves when they all went together the following Sunday.

After they started attending The Little Church, Mother arranged for a Memorial Service for Father and after Mother died, Harry did the same for her.

At the first service, there were just the five of them; at the second, just the four. The minister held both in the requiem chapel, behind the organ and the choir stall.

And so, though the memory of The Little Church was forever tinted with sorrow, Lou had come to feel about it much as Mother had felt years earlier when she had chanced upon it: coming there she felt a kind of comfort, felt closer to Mother and the boys, felt – as Mother had – that the words at the base of the statue of Jesus were intended for her.

Come Unto Me and I Will Give You Rest.

It was Lou's habit to arrive each Sunday half an hour before Service so she could sit in the pew they had all shared in those earlier years, and when she closed her eyes, listening to the music, listening to the minister, she could imagine Mother and Harry kneeling to her left, Norman and David to her right. She had, on occasion, been almost certain she could smell Mother's perfume, hear the boys intoning their prayers.

> Blessed Lord, grant that we
> May embrace and ever hold
> Fast the blessed hope
> Of life everlasting

Lou wondered, that winter Sunday, about the nature of Life Everlasting: wondered whether Mother and Father had been reunited beyond the grave, were now at play in the fields of the Lord.

She imagined those fields to be bathed in light – such as streamed through the stained-glass windows of The Little Church – imagined Mother and Father revealing to each other all the secrets – joys and sorrows – of their hearts.

She felt, especially when she was in The Little Church, that they could look down and see her, see the boys as well – wherever they might be – and were keeping watch over them, keeping them all safe until one day they could all be reunited in a better place than the earthly place they had shared for so short a time.

Lou often wondered in those early years alone in the city why it had been destined and determined that they should bear such a burden, endure such a sorrow. She wondered if she and the boys were paying the awful price for the sins of their ancestors. And thought of the words in Lamentations:

> Remember, O Lord, what
> > Happened to us
> We have become orphans
> Our Fathers have sinned and
> > Are no more
> And we bear their punishment

Lou wondered what their fathers must have done to incur such wrath, make God wreak his vengeance on four innocent children.

> Almighty God, give us grace
> That we may cast away
> The works of darkness

Lou could not recall ever giving in to the forces of darkness, nor could she imagine the boys ever having done so, and yet – and yet they had all been cast into the wilderness, into outer darkness, to cope as they might, without even the comfort of each other's presence.

If she ever got to Heaven – and it was her fervent sixteen-year-old hope she would get to Heaven and be reunited with her brothers and her parents never to be separated again – she hoped she would find out why, find out what they or their fathers had done to earn such a punishment.

> Thou shalt not kill
> Thou shalt not steal
> Thou shalt not bear false witness
> Thou shalt love thy neighbour as thyself.

Had they erred, inadvertently?

Had they committed – even unconsciously – some grievous sin?

Lou could recall nothing she had ever done or said, she or the boys.

And yet here they were, all alone in the world living their punishment, far far from home with no way of finding their way back.

> Joy is gone from our hearts
> Why do you always forget us?
> Why do you forsake us?

Lou had read and re-read Lamentations; felt she might have written those words herself, just as she might have written some of the lamentations of Job:

> God, tell me what charges
>> You have against me
> Does it please you
>> To oppress me?
> Will you turn now
>> And destroy me?
> Why did you bring me
>> Out of the womb?
> I wish I had died before
>> An eye saw me.

Like baby Thomas had died, and baby Margaret after him, dead in their cribs after Harry had been born but long before the advent of Norman and David and Lou.

It may have been a sign of some kind, an omen – one which Mother and Father ought to have heeded.

Lou wondered whether, like Job, she was now destined for that

> Land of gloom
>> And deep shadows

She could not imagine, could not bear to believe, that she might be.

> All the days of my hard service
> I will wait for my renewal
>> To come

It was Lou's fervent prayer.

> The joy of our hearts
>> Is ceased
> Our dance is turned
>> To mourning
> Wherefore dost thou
>> Forget us
>> Forever
> And forsake us?
> Remember our days
>> As of old

Lou's fervent prayer, and fear.
I hope God hasn't forgotten me.

Hm?
Benjamin stirred, sat up in the chair where he'd been dozing.
What did you say, Lou?
Nothing, said Lou. I think I was dreaming.
And a moment later, she was fast asleep again.

Lou was in her car, in the garage. It was a new car, a '52 Ford convertible, black with red leather seats, Robert's gift on their anniversary. Lou was in the driver's seat, with a wooden box in her lap. It was a long narrow box with a hinged lid, made of cherry wood. The lid was decorated with a flower – a daisy, Mother's favorite – stem and leaves. The flower was in raised relief, the lid having been carved out of a larger block of wood. On the face of the box were Mother's initials and, superimposed over them and contained within them, Father's. The box was Father's gift to Mother – a box for her rings and brooch and string of pearls, her precious things. A Christmas gift. His last, as it would turn out.

Lou lifted the lid. Inside the box was a tiny doll, primitive, made of pine. The head was a circle – about two inches in diameter – on which Father had penciled two button eyes and a button nose and a half-moon smile. Around the head was a halo of golden hair – pine shavings glued to the circumference of the circle. Lovely hair, Lou. Like yours. Not quite as nice, of course. But lovely just the same. The head was attached by a short bit of rope to the body – a triangle of pine, down the front of which Father had penciled three buttons and a belt, then some vertical lines to indicate the folds of a dress. Two scrawny rope legs.

Lou remembered the day Father had made the doll. They were in the garage of Grandfather's house in Ephrata. At the far end of the garage, furthest from the double doors, was Grandfather's workbench over which hung a hooded lamp and upon which were all sorts of tools. Father had lifted Lou and sat her on the workbench, beside the vice. In the vice was the lid of the box Lou now held on her lap. Father had finished the daisy, but not yet the leaves and the stem. Let's see, he said. I think I saw one of your dolls here, just a little while ago.

Which doll? she said.

Oh, he said. One of your favourites, I'm sure.

I don't see a doll, she said.

It's here somewhere, he said.

And ten minutes later, there it was, curls and all, in her hands.

What shall we call her? said Father.

Lou looked down at her doll and then, turning to her left, the lid of the box Father was making for Mother.

Daisy, she said.

Father laughed.

Of course, he said. Of course.

Lou lifted the doll from the box. Some of the beautiful golden hair had been lost to time, but Daisy was otherwise none the worse for forty years' wear. Lou held her up. She had a little difficulty bringing Daisy into focus. Wiped her eyes and looked again.

Oh, she said. Oh.

She put Daisy back in the box

Lou turned the key, started the car.

She lifted the lever beside the seat and lay back staring at the rafters, hugging Mother's jewellery box to her chest.

Oh, she thought, pushing her foot down on the accelerator.

The car thrummed.

Eight minutes past two.

Time dropping like water from the leaves after the rain.

The lunch was untouched.

Someone had left the lamp on, the fluorescent one just above the bed, the one that made Lou look jaundiced. Benjamin pulled the cord, switching it off.

Outside Lou's room, the janitor swabbed the floor in lazy S-motions, backing himself from the nurses' station to his bucket of grey and sudsless water. Distantly, there was the sound of nurses talking to patients; the television Barbie chattered away and behind it all there was the whispery white noise of the air-conditioning system, all of it interrupted now and then by Dolores' gurgling as she sat there in her easy chair beside the flotilla of wheelchairs.

Benjamin slid down in the chair, crossed his legs at the ankle, shut his eyes.

And a moment or two later, he was in the lobby of a hotel in Port Dover and the desk clerk handed him a note. Your wife called. She said to call as soon as you came in. Never mind what time.

He hadn't heard that tremulous tone in Kathleen's voice before.

Luther has died.

When?

This morning.

This morning?

We tried calling as soon as we found out, but you'd already left. Then I tried your cell phone, but you must have had it shut off.

Benjamin was in Port Dover doing a magazine piece on commercial fishing in Lake Erie. He'd been out on the lake with a man who had been working the nets for more than thirty years.

What happened?

Luther had had a heart attack. He'd got up early that morning – he and his friends had a seven-thirty tee-off time at the club – he'd showered and shaved and must have felt something, felt something was wrong. He'd sat on the chair beside the shower stall. Which was where Madge found him, chin to chest, hands folded in his lap, legs outstretched and crossed at the ankles; like he was having a little nap before getting up and getting dressed and getting on with his day.

Just like Luther.

Pardon?

Showered, shaved, presentable. Ever the gentleman.

Kathleen laughed, a tentative laugh.

What are the plans?

There are no plans. He didn't want a funeral. He wanted to be cremated. The funeral home people have already been there. The kids and I are going up this afternoon. So Madge won't be alone.

How is she?

She's fine. Seems fine. As fine as you'd expect. She's all right. At his age, it wasn't much of a shock – apart from suddenly finding him there.

I'll pack up and head home tonight.

Are you finished your story?

No. I was going to go out on the boat again tomorrow.

Stay. There's nothing for you to do. The funeral home people are handling everything. We'll do something, have a memorial or something, when you get home.

You sure? You sure you'll be all right?

Yes, said Kathleen. We're fine.

How are the kids?

They were a bit teary when we got the news. They were upset, but they seem fine now. No. You stay. We'll see you on the weekend.

They were quiet for a moment, then Kathleen said: Benjamin?

Yes.

How about you?

Me? I'm fine, said Benjamin. I'm all right.

You sure you're all right?

Yes, said Benjamin. I'm all right.

How are you feeling?

I'm feeling fine.

The truth of it was: he didn't know what he was feeling. Surprise, certainly. A mild shock. But apart from that?

So, Benjamin had stayed in Port Dover another two days, finished his research and headed home. The following week, a cloud-scudding, windblown day in September they boarded a yacht owned by one of Luther's long-time pals and headed up the bay to a spot just offshore from the country house – the house Luther had built and had loved more than any of the many others he had owned through the years – a house on a hill overlooking the bay which blued away to the northern horizon. Jack Scott turned the yacht and cut the engines so that they were drifting back down the bay toward town and Benjamin opened the urn and poured out some of Luther's ashes and handed the urn to Madge who emptied it and dropped it into the bay and then dropped a single yellow rose – one of Luther's favourites – into the water.

And that was that.

Well, said the nurse, what a pair of sleepyheads we have here.

Hm?

Excuse me. The nurse stepped over Benjamin's legs, removed the trash bag from Lou's night table, taped another in its place.

Lou stirred, opened her eyes, then closed them and drifted off again into the land of sleep and memory, far from this shore littered with wrecks, far from the meddlesome crew members. Sweet sailing, Lou.

Rilke hove into view, again.

> Who has turned us around this way
> > so that we're always
> > > whatever we do
> > in the posture of someone
> > > who is leaving?

And how did the rest of it go, that piece for the Elegies?

Something about a man standing on a hill, looking over the home valley one last time.

> That's how we live
> > always
> > > saying goodbye

Did she know that? Did she know this was goodbye? If so, she didn't seem overly perturbed or even overly conscious of the moment. Which surprised Benjamin. He had come expecting something other than this clock-ticking, whispery, sedate leave-taking. Had imagined something more dramatic, like those scenes in the movies where the wife and child come to visit one last time the man on death row: weeping and gnashing of teeth.

Benjamin looked at Lou's dentureless mouth.

Well, weeping anyway.

But no. Just this. Just this, which seemed to be, well, seemed to be just another visit which would soon conclude with a kiss on the cheek and – I'll be seeing you – except in this case the seeing would be done in another time and on another plane, if there was to be any seeing done at all. Of which Benjamin could not declare himself certain.

Perhaps Lou was right. Perhaps they all had a date with eternity. Which begged a question or two: what to do with all that time (although strictly speaking there wouldn't be any, time that is). There'd be no clocks, no days, no weeks, no months, no years, no markers down that vast eternity to tell you where you were in terms of past and future.

Seasons? One would hope so. The seasons were one of the highlights of his life, though for many people in many parts of the world there were no seasons, not with snow, anyway. So, seasons in eternity would come as a surprise, unsettling some of the saints. Couldn't have that.

Maybe they'd have it set up like a theme park: seasons, right this way. One of the wonders of the world. Step right up. See the leaves change colour right before your eyes.

So, yes, they would have seasons for those who wanted them. And, one would hope, they would have some of the other joys and comforts of this world: music, food, wine, a shady spot to sit and read which would, of course, demand books.

Or would they have books? Having passed through this dimension to the next, would we need to read at all? Would we suddenly find that all was revealed? All the knowledge we had been seeking, all the knowledge which had hitherto been withheld, kept secret. If so, why would we need books? There would be no further need to puzzle about the meaning of life, thus no need to consult psychological texts, or delve into the great novels and the poems which delve into the human condition.

Thus no Rilke. But what kind of Heaven would it be if there were no Rilke, no Chopin, no Malamud, no Tom Thomson. No striving for light and harmony and understanding.

What a cruelty. Finally to have all the time in the world to sit and listen to music, to sit and read books, to sit and stare at paintings and... nothing. What would people do? Souls do? Sit around and talk? Or would they just all lounge around in a constant state of bliss, like a bunch of stoned refugees from the sixties, humming along on a hand-painted tour bus with Ken Kesey doing the driving?

Wouldn't there have to be human seasons as well? Despair and sadness, fear and horror – all those ingredients which leaven the bread of life, which add dimension and richness to the joy we occasionally feel? If one were to be joyful forever, humming and whistling down the sunny streets of Paradise, how would one even recognize the fact unless there were shadows now and then, a good pelting thunderstorm, to remind us we were bathing in this brilliant light and warmth? Benjamin wasn't so certain.

God, look at her.

The one nurse nodded in the direction of the television, whose screen Benjamin, from his vantage point, could not quite see.

You look at some of these skinny kids and you wonder how they convince themselves that that's beautiful. The nurses shook their heads and went back to work.

Benjamin looked at Lou. What was left of her. Down from a summertime high of a hundred pounds to, what? Eighty? If that. Her upper arms not quite the width of three of Benjamin's fingers, side by side. Wasting away by the hour. So determined. And not the least bit weepy and sad. Glad to have her ticket. Anxious to hand it to The Boatman who will pole her over to the farther side. No wonder that, old and tired and worn, she was keeping an impatient eye on The Boatman who seemed to be idling around over there on the other shore, having another smoke, taking his own sweet time.

Benjamin guessed that, trading places, he'd be tapping his foot as well.

Perhaps, already, Lou has had a vision of what's over there on that other shore. Maybe the closer you get, the more of it that comes into view – as happens when you're taking the ferry from Leamington, say, to Pelee Island. First just a low hump on the Lake Erie horizon, then colour and the shape of trees, then details – the dead trees fingering out of the waters of the north-end swamp, the cone of the old stone lighthouse – then the ramp clanks down onto the wharf and there you are.

Maybe that was what it was like now for Lou. Maybe she could see people standing on the wharf, waiting for her: Robert and her brothers and her Mother and her Father and tail-wagging Chester and all the company of saints and angels in whom she had put her faith and her hope since she was a little girl and belief had been the only thing which had guided her through the sorrowful shoals of life on earth, her lonely orphan's life.

What must that have been like? To have lost, or lost touch with, the only people to whom you were related. To be left, except for Robert, utterly alone on the face of the planet.

Malamud knew:

> We live in mystery, a cosmos of separate lonely
> bodies, men, insects, stars. It is all a loneliness
> and men know it best.

She had known it. She had known it all her life, this woman with her amazing capacity for loving, for being loved. A capacity which had landed her where? Up on the shoals all by herself. This woman who ought to have had, who deserved to have had, children to get her through these last and lonely years.

What kind of cruel sick and twisted joke had that been, hm? Played upon her by a God whom she professed to love and to trust. Was it any wonder that once upon a time she had gone out to the garage, turned the key, leaned back and waited? Was it any wonder that, saved by a curious neighbour, waking in the white confines of a hospital room (which she had, for a moment, mistaken for Heaven) was it any wonder that she was utterly devastated?

The episode in Lou's garage and her life-long supply of anti-depressants were no surprise to Benjamin. What surprised him was that she was still here at all.

No wonder she had clung all her life to Robert. No wonder she had clung, since Robert's death, to Kathleen and Benjamin and the children.

Why didn't she have children? Kathleen had wondered on one of their summertime drives back to Canada.

Benjamin didn't know.

You never asked her?

No. He never had.

Kathleen wondered why.

How can you ask someone a question like that?

One word at a time.

As Kathleen had done, their very next visit.

It was Bob who hadn't wanted children. He'd never said as much, in so many words, but later – when it was too late – Lou had come to realize this fact about him.

At first, he had just wanted to wait.

Wait for what? Kathleen had wondered, and asked.

Wait until they were a little more established; wait until they had money in the bank, a down payment on a house, some furniture. Wait until we're a bit more comfortable, he said. Plausible enough. It would be hard enough to raise children, he thought, without the worry of money hanging over their heads. Child-rearing years should be joyous years, they shouldn't be clouded and gloomed over by his having to wonder where their next meal was coming from. When they had children – and he was always talking in those early years about having children – he wanted to be able to give them all the advantages he'd never had. He or Lou. He didn't want them wearing hand-me-downs; he didn't want them to have to miss out on activities or trips. He wanted to feed his children well, dress them well, send them to the best schools.

How could you disagree with that?

And so they had waited and Bob had squirreled away his money and they had bought a home and filled it with furniture and Lou had thought: perhaps now is the time.

Bob wasn't sure.

Bob was never sure.

By this time, he was the general manager of Erkelens – a year later he would be president and part owner of a company of his own, thanks to Luther Miles. Business matters preoccupied him. He wouldn't want to be an absentee father; he wanted to be there for his children in a way his own father had not been – all his children, three or four anyway. If only Lou could wait, be patient for another year, say. Two at the most.

Thus the years had passed, a kind of slow and measured unwinding of possibilities.

They settled into their routines and Bob wondered now and then, innocently almost, whether she was perfectly happy in their life together; whether she wanted for anything.

And she said no, she wanted for nothing. Except children.

But increasingly, she said this without feeling it; she had grown so accustomed to their freedom, their ability to come and go, take vacations when and where they wished, sit quietly in their quiet house and read together without any distractions. On those occasions when they came home from a visit to a house full of children, they collapsed into silence as soft as a pillow.

Bob always made a point of remarking how lovely the children had been, how lucky the parents, what good parents they were. But my, didn't Lou have a headache after all that noise? He certainly had a headache. Not that he didn't love children, don't get him wrong. He was looking forward to a house full of children some day; but he'd never stopped to think how noisy children could be, and how demanding; how little privacy you could have with children under foot; how little time you would have to sit and read, sit and think, be alone with your thoughts.

Still, it would be wonderful, wouldn't it, when they had children of their own? They would get used to all that.

Eventually, Lou wasn't certain.

Though Robert seemed as anxious as ever to have children, she found herself having doubts.

And finally, he began pressing her: the time has arrived, we really should begin a family, Lou; we're not getting any younger, we're both in our thirties. If we leave it any longer it could get very tricky. He brought home articles which explained at great length and gruesome detail the risks women took – with their own health and the health of their babies – if they waited past thirty; how the risks multiplied with each passing year until, by the time she was in her mid-thirties, the mother was almost guaranteed to harm her own health in childbirth and would almost certainly give birth to a child weakened in some mortal way: physically or psychologically or both.

Ultimately, it had been Lou who said no.

It had been Lou who had insisted, against Robert's pleading, that they would bring no children into this world, into this house.

They were too comfortable, too set in their ways, too happy with each other to risk their relationship being toppled into turmoil by the arrival of these little strangers in their midst.

It was then they had moved into separate bedrooms; she in the rear of the house, he in the front, there to spend the rest of their married nights in separate single beds.

In some ways, she said, we were more like brother and sister than husband and wife. Particularly in the latter years, when we had our own rooms. Odd at first. But then we settled into our routines and it felt very comfortable, very comforting. Uncomplicated, if you know what I mean.

Uncomplicated?

By sex.

Oh, he said.

Sex isn't everything, she said. I'm sure you know that by now yourself. And it isn't everything it's cracked up to be. In many ways, and I know this sounds strange to say so, we became closer after all that ended. There were no secrets between us. He was the one person to whom I could open my heart. There was nothing I couldn't tell him, nothing I was afraid to tell him. He was the one person I could trust completely.

Trust?

To listen, and to understand. He was a wonderful listener. I could tell him anything that was on my mind – however odd or fanciful – and I would know that he would never judge me or think ill of me, no matter what I thought or said. Being with him was like being embraced. At all times. No matter what. It seemed to me that as we got older and settled into the rhythms of our lives – in many ways separate and solitary lives – we actually became closer. I know it sounds strange, or peculiar, but it's true.

There's a wonderful line in Rilke, he said. Perhaps you know it.

> Love consists in this. That two solitudes
>
> greet, border and protect each other.

That's precisely how I felt, she said.

Some couples, he said, are exactly the opposite: smother each other or, more likely, smother the other. I know people like that. Couples like that. One in particular: he can't go to the hardware without her tagging along. Everywhere he goes, she goes. She makes as though it's only because they're especially close and still, after all these years, in love. But I have my doubts. It's as though she's afraid that if she lets him out of her sight, he'll just keep on going. Like that story about the guy who takes the garbage out and never comes back. If I were him, that's exactly what I'd do, just to get away from her, get his life back. I don't know why people do that to each other.

Our of fear, I suspect. Fear or insecurity, she said. But if you love someone, that's the last thing you should want or need to do. Drape yourself all over them, hang from their arm like some love-struck teenager. If you really love someone you should set them free. Isn't that what they say? Set them free to be who they are and who they want to be, not to try to force the other person into an image of your own making.

Not easy to do, he said.

No, she said.

And it's weird, isn't it? A woman marries someone because she loves him and then as soon as she marries him she sets out to change him.

Sad, she said, that some people succeed. They want to change the other person, and they do change that person. They succeed so completely that the other person is no longer someone they know, or like.

How could you like him? He'd be a different person than the person you married. And he couldn't help but resent the person who'd forced him to change.

I think he'd blame himself. Blame himself for failing to be true to himself. I know men like that, she said. Men who have caved in to their wives, gradually left behind the things – hobbies and habits – that their wives didn't like. Finally became the man their wife wanted them to be. And then wound up not recognizing the man in the mirror. How would you feel about yourself, if you let that happen?

And how would you feel about her? Benjamin wondered.

How else could you feel? You'd resent her.

I think you'd really resent yourself. For being untrue to yourself. For going along in the first place. Agreeing to become this other person.

You're right, she said. But it's her you'd want to take it out on. And so the whole enterprise would just backfire. She'd succeed in changing you, just as she'd hoped to do, but in the end she'd lose you. And she probably wouldn't end up liking the person she'd created. Like, or respect him. How could you? How could you respect someone who wasn't true to himself? So you'd fail, because you'd succeeded.

Lou's riddle, he said. He smiled and nudged her arm.

She laughed and nudged him back. Somehow, she said, we managed to avoid all that.

Same with us, said Benjamin. That's one of the things I love about Kathleen. She's just let me be me. Although there were times, particularly at the beginning, when she tried to tweak me here and there, rearrange me into someone a little more respectable.

She didn't have much luck, did she?

No, he said. I guess she didn't.

Lucky you.

Yes, he said. Lucky me. And lucky us.

I was just happy to be with Robert, she said. And he with me. It sounds so sappy to say so, but it was perfect. Really. As perfect as could be.

And the years had wound down.

Robert sounded, Kathleen thought, very clever.

Yes, said Lou. He was clever. Very clever. Very convincing. Very determined.

And very manipulative.

Yes, said Lou. I suppose he was, but...

But what? Kathleen wanted to know.

It wasn't his fault, entirely. He had his reasons for not wanting children. But he wasn't a tyrant. And I wasn't a victim. I don't want to leave you with that impression. If I'd really wanted children, we'd have had children. I let myself be convinced. I was a willing partner.

You knew what he was doing?

Oh yes, said Lou. I know, and I knew then.

But you wanted children. You've said so dozens of times.

Yes, said Lou. Yes, I have.

Didn't you mean that?

On one level, certainly. It would have been lovely. But on another level, it was just as easy not to have them. Much of what Robert said was true: about what children would have done to our lives. We had become creatures of routine, both of us. And as much as children would have been wonderful, it became obvious we were enjoying our lives just the way they were. And I had my reasons, as well, for wanting things to stay as they were.

What reasons?

Reasons, said Lou, politely closing that particular door.

Robert was a charming man.

They met in New York: Lou was working as a receptionist for Fidelity Life and Robert had walked in through the door and into her life one sunny September afternoon. This would have been the year she turned twenty: 1935.

He looked like a boy in men's clothing, scrubbed and buffed, his face slightly flushed from his hurrying to get to the appointment, fearing he would be late. He was wearing a navy double-breasted suit –

no stripes, very conservative, not like the Robert he was to become – and his brogues glistened as he entered the waiting room and then stopped to get his bearings. He removed his black fedora and approached the desk behind which Lou sat, her heart thrumming curiously. She remembers hoping she wasn't blushing – Robert said later he didn't think she had been or, in his own nervousness, perhaps he just hadn't noticed. His fedora hung from his fingertips. Piano hands was the thing she would remember: long, thin, carefully-manicured fingers which looked capable of dancing magically over a keyboard.

Robert introduced himself and Lou excused herself to alert Mister Ryback to the fact that Robert Copeland had arrived, somewhat early, for an interview pertaining to employment. Mister Ryback asked that Mister Copeland make himself comfortable. He would send for him in a moment or two. The moment or two had turned into nearly twenty; Robert sitting, then standing, then pacing, then sitting, careful not to crease his trousers when he crossed his legs at the knee.

He had won the job, of course – how could anyone not hire such an eager beaver on the spot – and then two weeks later he and Lou had gone out for their first lunch and, two months after that she was wearing Robert's mother's engagement ring.

The first Saturday in April of 1936 they exchanged their vows before God, two friends from the office and the minister of The Little Church; had supper at Toots Shor's on West 51st then took a cab to Grand Central Station and by midnight were snuggled in each other's arms in a roomette the size of a closet as the train hurtled through the night to Washington for a weekend honeymoon, all they could afford, time or money.

That was it for Lou's job, of course: the company had a policy. It would not employ married couples. Which was neither here nor there: Robert had his own married-couples policy. No wife of his was ever going to have to lift a finger working for someone else. Which was fine by Lou: she'd never liked the job or Mister Ryback all that much to begin with, would much rather stay home, turning the studio apartment into the home she'd been dreaming of all these years.

Oh, those early days.

How she treasured the memories.

Each day, at lunch hour, she met Robert at the front door of Fidelity Life. They walked the three blocks to Danny's Deli where they'd become a fixture. Danny's was a hole-in-the-wall on 43rd, tile floors, tin ceilings, with booths on the left and a long counter on the right where Danny and his short-order cooks prepared the food. As they walked in the door, Danny yelled hello – he was always yelling, yelling and laughing, trading insults with customers – and Brenda the waitress was heading for their booth in the bar corner, two glasses of milk balanced on one upturned palm.

How are the little lovebirds today?

After lunch, they walked the neighbourhood streets, shopping the windows, browsing in stores occasionally – especially in winter when the wind keened through those midtown canyoned streets – then they would head back to Fidelity Life so that Robert could be at his desk working, a minute or two before the appointed time of one o'clock. Mister Ryback was an eagle.

After she'd kissed him goodbye, watched him into the elevator, gave him one last wave as the doors slid shut between them, Lou idled her way home – sometimes stopping to spend an hour in a bookstore or a department store – and then busied herself preparing the evening meal. She was an expert cook – she could thank Aunt Willa for that – and nothing pleased her quite so much as having the table prepared – candles and flowers – and food on its way from the oven to the table the moment she heard Robert's key in the lock.

He was forever bringing her flowers or other little surprises – small gifts (a brooch, a book of poems) which had caught his eye as he'd passed one shop or another. And he was forever grateful for the warm little nest she was making for them, high above the sirened streets of Manhattan.

A hopeless romantic, that was Robert.

Kathleen had another view, which Benjamin urged her to keep to herself.

Give me a little credit, said Kathleen, arching an eyebrow.

The nurse's aide startled him. Sorry, she said. It's all right, he said, I was just daydreaming. He yawned and checked the time: two thirty-nine. Time for a nap, he said. The woman laughed. You fit right in with the rest of them, then. And she laughed again. You keep that up, we may have to keep you. We haven't got no Canadians. You'd be a prize possession. She extended her hand. I'm Angela. I'm her favourite. She turned to Lou. Aren't I?

Aren't you what?

Your favourite.

My favourite what?

Ooooo. Wake up like a bear, Lou. Grrrr. Angela made a show of her teeth, then broke into a smile. She lifted the lid covering one of the dishes on Lou's lunch tray. Comin' on supper time and ain't even et dinner. She shook her head then looked at Lou. Still not eatin'?

Apparently not, said Lou.

Oooooeeee. Angela shook her head and picked up the tray. She's a wilful one, that's for certain. Benjamin nodded in agreement. Wilful would be the word all right. Angela took the tray out to the trolley in the hall and, a moment later, came back in. Lucille? Angela put a hand on Lou's shoulder, gave her a gentle shake. How 'bout we get you up out of that bed and into your Rolls Royce so your young man came all the way from Canada can take you for a spin. How 'bout that?

Lou mumbled something. No, in all likelihood.

Excellent, said Angela. She lowered the safety rail and moved Lou's ankles toward the edge of the bed.

Leave me be.

No leavin' you be now, honey. Time to rise and shine.

I don't want to get up.

You got to get up, Lou. Half the day's gone. You got a visitor. You bein' rude as a wet kiss. You got to get up honey. You can't lay there in bed all day. You gonna turn into one giant bedsore you do that. She put her arm beneath Lou's shoulder and the next thing Lou knew, she was sitting up. Not very pleased, but sitting up.

You need help?

Angela looked at Benjamin with a bemused smile. Me? She shook her head. I'm an old farm girl from Loseeanna. Ain't nothin I can't handle around here. But thanks for the offer. And sure enough, a couple of minutes later, there was Lou, hunched in her wheelchair, arms crossed before her chest, wearing a look like sour milk.

Is there some law against a person doing as she wishes?

No, said Angela. 'Cept if you wish to do what I don't want you to do.

And who elected you Queen of the Ward?

Angela laughed and gave Lou's shoulder a gentle rub. I don't think getting into a wheelchair is going to be the end of you Lou.

I wish it were that easy.

Silence.

Benjamin took Lou for a turn around the nurses' station, then parked her for a moment in front of the television.

You feeling like watching a show?

No.

You still watch your favourites?

No

Do they ever show movies here?

No.

Remember our movie nights?

It had been their habit, Lou's and Kathleen's and Benjamin's, to rent movies from the classics section – Bette Davis movies were their favourites (Dangerous, Jezebel and Dark Victory most especially) – make popcorn in the microwave and sit around Lou's living room until they couldn't stop yawning.

Lou had declared movie nights her favourite nights of the year, could hardly wait from visit to visit so they could go down to the video store and browse the shelves, then go home and sit together and watch the movies which Lou had first seen in the theatres with Robert all those years ago.

Benjamin wondered if Lou would like to take a little trip.

A trip where?

Oh... maybe down to the far end of the building.

Lou was silent.

Silence equals assent. Or so they say.

He started pushing the wheelchair. Lou didn't complain. Didn't say anything.

Just past the nursing station, they took a right turn and headed down the corridor which led to the craft room on the left and the dining room on the right. The oldsters were all lined up along the right side of the corridor, from just beyond the nursing station all the way to the closed double doors of the dining room: the front of one wheelchair nuzzled up against the back of the one ahead in line.

What are they all lined up for?

Supper, said Lou.

What time's supper?

Not until five-thirty.

Benjamin checked his watch: Seven past three.

That's two and a half hours away. And they're lined up already?

Some of them start lining up right after lunch.

Why?

Nothing else to do. Or maybe they're afraid there won't be any room for them if they're late.

Aren't there enough tables?

There's a spot for everyone, said Lou. The tables are all assigned.

Hm.

Hm, indeed, said Lou.

Most of those who were lined up and waiting did not seem to be aware they were lined up and waiting. In fact, most of them didn't seem to be aware of anything. But this was not quite the case, for as Benjamin pushed Lou past the line of the waiting, one of them – a man with a tuft of white hair standing atop an otherwise bald head – glared at them angrily and said in a kind of growl: this is the front of the line. The back of the line is back there. He indicated the back of the line with an angry jerk of his thumb. Benjamin smiled and nodded, before catching the drift of what the old man was saying. We're just…

No cutting in, said the man.

Yes, said a woman a couple of wheelchairs back. Don't try cutting in.

Nurse! said another.

We're not cutting in, said Benjamin. He was on the brink of saying: this woman doesn't care about the dining room; she's not interested in eating. In fact, she's in the process of starving herself to death. So help yourself, eat your dinner and hers as well. It won't bother her at all. But instead he said: we're just going for a ride.

Yah, said the tufted man. I bet.

Yah, said the woman two wheelchairs back.

I'll be watching you, said the man.

So will I, said the woman.

Nurse!

Benjamin rolled Lou past the dining room doors, past another nursing station at the far end of the hall and then made a right turn into what turned out to be a dead-end corridor of private and semi-private rooms. The only sound in the carpeted corridor was the murmur of the building's air conditioning and, somewhere not far off, a faint mechanical beeping. In the rooms they passed Benjamin could see the traces of lives lived: bookshelves, favourite armchairs, desks with lamps, framed photos of loved ones hanging on the walls. Galleries of familiar faces smiling down upon the lone occupants of these rooms. Little traces of lives lived, of lives lost. And Benjamin could not help but think of the eventual and inevitable contracting nature of our lives.

He and Lou reached the far end of the corridor, turned and made their slow way back: passing the room of one old soul after another, each clinging to the flotsam of lives lived beyond the point of usefulness. Lou didn't seem to notice, seemed to be keeping her eyes on the corridor in front of them. Perhaps through lack of interest. Perhaps through force of will. Perhaps for the better.

A few minutes later they were back where they'd started, heading toward the oldsters lined up against the wall, waiting to be rolled to the dining room. Was it any wonder Lou didn't want to wait in that lineup? Was it any wonder she'd decided to jump that queue?

And here they were – three-nineteen, elapsed time about twelve minutes – back in the television corner near the nurses' station: Move, said Pink Slacks, left or right. One way or the other. The women in front of her gaped at the screen and did not respond, perhaps did not hear her, perhaps did not comprehend, perhaps understood but were powerless to respond; perhaps were beyond caring. The complainer sitting on the couch seemed quite capable of getting up and moving so as to get a better view of the screen but she did not move, just reiterated her demand, more content to be annoyed than to see what was on the television. Move...

A few feet away, mouth yawning, gums exposed, eyes glazed, Dolores sat in her recliner, long gray hair over the shoulders of her red-and-white patterned robe, a hand-made beige wool afghan over her lap.

Could she hear?

Could she see?

Could she think of all that once was and was no more? Could she recall all that she once had, all that had slipped through her arthritic fingers and dropped beyond reach and sight? Where were all those who once upon a happier time had been caressed by the fingers before those fingers had become so disfigured? Where were all those who once upon a time had been kissed by those lips, now so thin and chapped and colourless? Where were all those who once upon a time had fallen within the loving gaze of those hazel eyes? Where was the hand to smooth her hair, the way she had once smoothed the hair of those she loved? Had she outlived them all? Or had she merely out-lived their affection? Or had they all simply turned away, their hearts breaking at the sight of her? Benjamin turned away. But turning away didn't quite do the trick. Dolores had burrowed into his memory. He had the feeling she would be visiting him in the middle of many nights to come. She and Lou. And the others. The others who wait.

Benjamin thought of that quip about Florida, and God's waiting room. God had more than one. God was a very busy fellow. It would take Him a while to get around to all his waiting rooms, all those who patiently – or otherwise – waited in them.

What was it Lou had said? About God forgetting?

Benjamin was relieved to think he had a few more years before he joined this crowd at the gate. Though who knows? Not quite two months earlier, a forty-seven-year-old friend of his had dropped to the floor of the courtroom during a flourishing defence of his client. Dropped and could now be found, face contorted, words garbled, left side paralyzed, sitting in a wheelchair in a nursing home. So who's to know? All things considered, Benjamin would rather drop like a stone. Now you see him, now you don't. He was comforted by the knowl-edge that both his parents had dropped from sight in precisely that way. All things considered, he'd rather not be winched out of his bed by an E-Z Lift and deposited in a wheelchair, then rolled out to some lobby to sit and drool the day away.

I'd like to go to my room now.
Sure.
And a few minutes later, three thirty-four, with the help of a pass-ing nurse, there she was back where he'd found her, lying on her side

on her bed with her back to him, her blanket pulled to her shoulder and held in place by the fingers of her left hand.

Benjamin sat once more in the chair beside the bed, staring at Lou's back.

And now, six more of the top one hundred hits from 1967.

Number Twenty-Four.

The Rolling Stones.

Ruby Tuesday.

And Benjamin, shutting his eyes, was in the little hospital at the top of the hill in Southampton.

Grandmother Miles was in a private room on the ground floor – lights off, fan humming. It took her a moment, rising from sleep, to recognize him. Benjamin!

How are you?

I'm dying, said Grandmother, and took Benjamin's hand in hers and placed it on her abdomen: a tumor the size of a football.

How long has that been there?

Six months.

Six months?

Six or eight.

And you never thought to call the doctor?

Oh yes, said Grandmother. I called.

You called?

Pretty well as soon as I noticed it.

And?

And he said it was a tumor, which any idiot could have guessed.

And?

He laid out my options.

Which were?

To do something, or not.

And you chose the not?

I chose to enjoy my last few months, rather than vomiting and watching my hair fall out.

But, why…

It wasn't a difficult choice, Benjamin. There's almost no chance I would have survived this. It's a particularly nasty little tumor.

It's not so little.

No. Not any more.

How long have they given you?

Another week or two. Maybe three.

Have you talked with Father?

She shook her head. But I told his secretary.

His secretary?

Miss Dalton. Madge is her name. She called yesterday.

Madge?

I told your Father I was in hospital for a couple of tests and he apparently asked Miss Dalton to arrange to send some flowers – Grandmother half rolled in her bed. So she sent the flowers and then decided to visit since your Father is in Nashville, or Knoxville, or wherever. She's coming tomorrow.

Oh, said Benjamin.

Oh what?

Nothing, said Benjamin.

They talked for a while: Grandmother asking him about Mother, and his schooling, then Benjamin made his excuses, stifling a yawn, said he was going to check on the house, make sure everything was all right.

You'll find liquor in the usual spot.

He did. And some Cuban cigars in the humidor. And he later fell softly into sleep, the lake lapping onto the beach a few hundred feet from the bedroom window.

In the morning: Benjamin? This is Miss Dalton. Madge. Your Father's secretary.

Miss Dalton couldn't have been more than thirty, and couldn't have been more surprised than when Grandmother made the introductions. She stood, colouring a little, and offered her hand.

Pleased, said Benjamin. I'm sure.

They made small talk for half an hour and then: I'll leave you ladies to your visit. I'm sure you've got lots to talk about.

Benjamin kissed his Grandmother goodbye.

I'll be back soon.

I wouldn't wait all that long, Benjamin.

How was she? Mother had wanted to know, then wanted to know what was on his mind.

She's dying.

I gathered that, said Mother. And?

And Benjamin told her about Father's secretary.

Secretary?

Miss Dalton.

Oh, said Mother.

Oh what?

Oh, that's her name, said Mother. And turned and left the room and went upstairs, gently shutting the door of her bedroom.

In the morning, Benjamin found her, sitting at the kitchen table, slippers and robe, a DuMaurier in one hand, glass of whiskey in the other.

Mother?

Join me in a drink?

He had, and by noon they had finished half the bottle and Mother had brought Benjamin up to speed on the state of affairs.

Literally.

In short, Miss Dalton may have been somebody's secretary, but was not Father's. Secretary, that is.

Oh.

So that's that, said Mother.

And that was that.

And two months later, Benjamin heard her bedroom door open, heard her footsteps on the stair, heard her rummaging around the kitchen for kettle and cup, drifted back to sleep.

Half past seven he'd heard her. Just past eight he found her – kettle whistling wildly on the stove – sprawled on the pine-board kitchen floor.

And no amount of crying, no amount of calling her name, no amount of telling her he loved her, no amount of holding her cooling hands in his would bring her back from the darkness – the vast and frightful darkness – into which she'd tumbled when no one was looking, when no one was there, to save her.

And Benjamin was later to wonder whether it was at that moment

– that long moment of waiting alone with Mother's hand in his, waiting for the ambulance, then the police, then the people from the funeral home, whether it had been at that moment he had begun to hate his Father.

Perfidious Father.

Father, who had betrayed Mother and had broken her heart, Father who had blithely gone his way – was having breakfast in the dining room of the Queen Elizabeth Hotel in Montreal – as his wife fell into darkness and Benjamin, too young, far too young, heard for the first time the laughter which echoes up out of such darkness – laughter of the goat-god – laughter which chilled his young heart.

It seemed to him that he had never again been warm, never in all the years of his youth, never in all the years of his young manhood, never until he met Kathleen. And even then, huddled before the warmth of a wife and a daughter and a son, face warm, face and hands, the cold ran its finger up his spine.

Even now.

Lou sighed and turned.

She was sitting before the mirror in the bedroom she shared with Mother. It was evening, just before bedtime. Lou was sitting on the bench, facing the mirror. Mother stood behind her, brushing her hair. One hundred strokes each night before bed. You have the most beautiful hair, Lou. It is a great gift. Another stroke, then another. Sixty-two. Sixty-three. If you do this every night, said Mother, your hair will always be lustrous, always beautiful.

Mirror mirror
on the wall
who's the fairest
of them all?

Mother smiled. You have the loveliest hair, Lou. Such a treasure. Her hair was Lou's pride. And Mother's pride as well.

When I was a girl, said Mother, I had beautiful hair too. Not as beautiful as yours, but lovely just the same. My Mother told me what I'm telling you: to brush it every night. One hundred strokes per night.

And I did, for many years. But then I missed a night here, and a couple of nights there, and got out of the habit of caring for it. And eventually, it lost its lustre and there was no getting it back. It was like all good gifts: if you fail to care for it, you'll lose it. Something to remember, Lou. Don't make my mistake. Cherish the gifts you've been given. They'll last a lifetime.

Mother's mistake was not a mistake Lou made. Each night, she took up Mother's brush – she still had that brush somewhere – and worked at her hair. Eighty-two. Eighty-three. One hundred strokes per night.

> Mirror mirror,
> on the wall,
> who's the fairest
> of them all?

When she married, it was Robert who stood behind her, working Mother's brush.

Thirty-six. Thirty-seven.

Why one hundred strokes? he wanted to know.

Because Mother said so.

Oh, he said.

Forty-three. Forty-four.

Maybe we should cut your hair, said Robert. Cut it and sell it. Like in that story. Remember that story?

The Gift? said Lou.

Yes, he said. He was smiling. It was meant as a joke.

Even so, a shudder passed through Lou at the thought of it.

Sell your gifts at your peril, she said.

And then one summer's evening, six years after they were married, Robert standing behind her as she sat facing the mirror: Oh, he said.

Lou's heart thrummed at the tone in his voice.

He held out the brush.

A great clump of Lou's lustrous hair held in its bristles.

And the next day another. And another.

Alopecia, said the doctor.

Oh, said Lou.

It's a condition, he said, where patches of hair are suddenly lost in a certain area.

Will it grow back? Lou wondered.

It may, said the doctor. It depends.

Upon?

It will depend on whether the hair loss continues.

Continues?

If you continue to lose more hair, it could be quite serious. It's what we call Alopecia universalis.

Which is?

Total loss of hair.

Total?

Over the entire body.

In which case?

In which case it's quite unlikely to grow back. We'll have to wait, he said. Wait and see.

Lou waited and saw, each night, another clump of her hair in the bristles of the brush until, when she returned to the doctor three weeks later, she had not a hair on her head or on her body.

Oh, said the doctor.

What causes this, she wondered?

We really don't know, he said. It's something of a medical mystery.

But not a mystery to Lou.

Lou had read her Bible.

She had read Obadiah:

> The pride of your heart
> has deceived you
> .. though you soar like an eagle
> and make your nest among the stars
> from there I will bring you down.

She had read Proverbs 8:

> I hate pride and arrogance

She had read Proverbs 11:

> When pride comes, then comes disgrace

She had read Proverbs 16:

> Pride goeth before destruction,
> A haughty spirit before a fall

She had read Proverbs 29:

> A man's pride brings him low.

Had read, but perhaps had not paid sufficient attention. Had read, but not understood.

It's not a punishment, said the doctor.

The doctor was entitled to his view.

Lou had, and has, her own.

Lou sighed again, and turned.

And Benjamin sighed at the sight of her. What was left of her.

So much of his adult life was linked with the life of this old woman. She was the only person now alive who knew his parents, knew him as a child, knew the places and the sounds and the look of that distant time and those distant places. Sitting there with her, talking with her of those times, he was carried back to his childhood, to a time he otherwise might not recall without the spontaneous springing up of memory when those old chords were struck, those old resonances recalled.

This, he thought, this is what I will lose when I lose her: the last tenuous link to my childhood, my past.

It would be like losing his Mother all over again, except that Mother had dropped from his life the way a hanged man drops through a trap door.

He was reminded of something Lou had once said in one of their lakeside chats: I can remember my Mother saying that some people are left behind, left to wait, to suffer, for a reason.

Which had led Benjamin to say that didn't sound like the way a loving God would treat the faithful.

Maybe they weren't quite as faithful as they thought they were, or they should have been. And let's not forget that God has his darker and more vengeful side: locusts and boils and pillars of salt.

And floods, said Benjamin.

Yes, said Lou. Let's not forget about the floods.

It was a gentle hand which woke him half an hour later – six minutes past four– a hand gripping his right shoulder, giving him a little shake. Benjamin?

Hm?

Benjamin looked up at the smiling face of Dorothy Fullum. I must have been nodding off.

You two make a good pair. Too bad I didn't have my camera.

Benjamin sat up, then stood. Must be the lack of air. Or – he looked down at Lou – maybe it's just catching.

Dorothy laughed. I've come to rescue you again. Would you like to go to Lou's apartment?

And a few minutes later, on the third floor of the far wing of the seniors' complex, there they were outside the door of Lou's apartment. Dorothy unlocked the door and opened it, reached in and flipped on the light.

Benjamin looked at Lou's little apartment, then turned to look at Dorothy. I feel as if I've come from a funeral. It's only four months, four or five, since we moved her in here. She seemed so happy. So content.

Sometimes it's like that. Sometimes they try to convince themselves that this will work out fine for them. They do try. But then after a while it just hits them that their life is over. Their old life. And the new life doesn't seem sturdy enough to support them and they sort of collapse. It happens more often than you think. But you're right. It is sad. Dorothy shook her head, managed a little smile. I've got to go see other patients. Can you find your way back okay, or do you want me to send someone to take you there?

No, said Benjamin. I'll find my way back.

Dorothy removed Lou's door key from her key ring and gave it to Benjamin. You can just leave this with the nurses when you're done. She extended her hand. It's been good meeting you, Benjamin. I'm just sorry we had to meet under these circumstances.

Dorothy turned to go, then turned back. Did you fly down, or drive? I flew.

If there are things you'd like us to keep until you can come back to get them, we have a storage area in the basement. We can keep things there for you until you can come back with your vehicle. You could just leave a note on the things you want to keep. I'll make sure they get to storage. Then we'll have someone come and take away the rest. Benjamin thanked her and shook her hand again. And then, click of the door, there he was, alone in Lou's little apartment.

Apartment was a bit of a stretch. It was really a room – more or less like a motel room: a short corridor leading from the front door to the main room. On the right side of the corridor there were two sets of sliding doors concealing floor-to-ceiling closets into which Benjamin had shoved all the boxes that, last spring, Lou had not been able to bring herself to leave behind: snapshot albums and shoeboxes filled with Christmas cards dating back half a century, shoes and sweaters, Bob's bowling and golf trophies, candle holders and teacups, place mats and silver napkin rings and a host of things which absolutely could not be sent to charity or the dump.

The previous May at Lou's old house it had taken them two days – Lou sitting in her favourite armchair, Benjamin and Kathleen bringing box after box – to make those choices: this goes to the dump, this goes to The Home.

Now and then Lou had held things in her hand for a final few minutes before shaking her head and sighing, relegating it to the garbage. My Lord, she said, these things we collect over the course of a lifetime. Look at this! Sitting at her feet was a cardboard box which Benjamin had dragged out from beneath her bed, a box filled nearly to the top with neatly-typed notes on three-ring paper. These are the records of our bowling league. They must date back to the 1950s. Maybe earlier. Why on earth would I have saved those?

Beats me, said Benjamin.

But their reprieve was at an end.

Garbage, said Lou, and out they'd gone, pitched unceremoniously into the dumpster after all those years safely hiding under the bed.

It had been horrible to force her to do it, to make all those final choices, and there were times during those two days in May when Benjamin couldn't bear to look at her, her eyes red-rimmed and brimming, had ducked out back to look at the sky, instead. And at the end of it all, there was the residue of her life, in boxes and garbage bags, out in the dumpster in the driveway.

Well, most of her life. The rest of it – the boxes which absolutely had to make the twelve-block trip from house to Home – they'd piled in the back seat and trunk of Benjamin's car. The same boxes which were now, despite Lou's care and determination, destined for the dump after all. Benjamin slid shut the closet doors.

He stepped in to the bathroom and flipped the light switch: an elevated toilet seat with safety handles, sink beside which there was an emergency call switch. Lou's soaps had gone dry in the rubber dish beside the faucets of the sink and the tub. He shut the light.

The bed-sitting room was about sixteen by twenty. It smelled of Murphy Oil and air freshener – the benefit of Lou being on the A Plan which included, for a moderate monthly fee, a thorough cleaning and dusting of every nook and cranny.

Lou's bed was on the left. At the foot of the bed, against the wall, was her bureau, topped with doilies upon which she'd placed some framed photographs: one of Robert shouldering his golf clubs standing by the yawning trunk of an Oldsmobile circa 1956; one of Benjamin and Kathleen and the kids smiling outside Lou and Robert's house one sunny summer day (the kids about eight and ten by the looks of it), one showing a couple of long-dead relatives looking grimly at the camera. Wedged into the corner was a straight-back chair with a hand-stitched seatcover depicting a hunting scene – deer bounding over a low wall, hunter and dog in pursuit – and behind the chair a standup lamp, one of three Lou had salvaged from her home.

Centred against the window-wall was Lou's rosewood desk, a gift from Robert in the year of their marriage, not a scratch on it anywhere, even after all these years, its brass handles still shiny, the gold filigreed leather writing surface just like new. This is why I love writing letters by hand, Lou once told him, running her fingers across the leather surface. She told him to sit, take a piece of writing paper and her favourite fountain pen and try for himself. She was right: the leather gave just slightly under the pressure of the nib: sensuous. Whoever would have thought of that in the first place? I've often wondered. It was no wonder she treasured that desk all through her life, rubbing and buffing it with oil and polish. And no wonder it was the first of Lou's things upon which Benjamin placed a stick-it note: Save For Benjamin Miles.

At the right corner of the desk stood a brass lamp with a dark-green shade. All across the back edge of the desk, nearest the windowsill, were some of Lou's essential books, her helpers: an Oxford dictionary, Roget's Thesaurus, a dictionary of proverbs, two copies of Walden, selected poems of Wordsworth, Bulfinch's Mythology, Bartlett's Familiar Quotations, Fowler's Modern English Usage, a dictionary of synonyms and antonyms, a book of great quotations, and a small leather-bound, zipper-cased King James edition of the Bible.

131

There were three drawers on the right and on the left a door which swung open to reveal a pull-out shelf upon which Lou kept her Smith-Corona portable typewriter. If ever he was to write the story of Lou's life, he thought, he would type it at this desk and on that typewriter. He cleaned out the drawers and put the papers and the typewriter in a box: Save For Benjamin Miles.

To the right of the desk, in the corner, was the television she and Benjamin had bought last May. Next to it, her record player, one of those 1940s RCA Victor models. It looked to be made of walnut. Open the hinged lid, there was the turntable. On the front there was a cloth-screen grille concealing the speaker. At the bottom was storage space for her 78s: Sinatra, Perry Como, Tony Bennett, Chopin, Beethoven, Bach. To the right of the record player there were two of Lou's yellow-cloth armchairs separated by a circular table upon which were two framed photos – one of Robert alone, standing before the fireplace, apparently on Christmas morning; the other of Lou and Robert standing on the shore of a lake, somewhere up north from the looks of it.

On the wall above her armchairs and bed were photographs which, taken together, constituted a kind of gallery of her life. On the wall at the head of Lou's bed was their wedding photo: Lou slim and shapely in a white business suit and matching pillbox hat, Robert in a three-piece suit – it looks black, but it was navy blue. And then, in no particular order: photographs showing Lou and her parents, her parents singly, her parents together, her parents with Lou and her brothers, her Mother alone with all the children (that was the summer Father died), some very old photos of relatives of both Lou and Robert, a shot of Chester the dog flopped down on the grass outside the farmhouse in New Jersey, a large frame containing ten photographs of Benjamin and Kathleen and the children, a photo framed by itself showing Robert holding a tiny Aaron in the crook of his arm, aiming a bottle at Aaron's mouth (that was the first time Robert had ever held a baby).

It had taken Benjamin the better part of an afternoon (I think that one should go over there .. no perhaps to the left of that one ..) to hang all those pictures in the order Lou thought best. And all that afternoon Lou had talked to him of her life, using the photographs on the wall and the snaps in her album as channel markers down the river of her past.

It was, she finally said, a very happy life, though certainly not without its sadnesses and its sorrows. But what was sorrow if not a kind of leavening.

All her life, Lou had kept journals. Shorthand notes of the days of her life: a shorthand no one but Lou could easily decipher but which – retrieving one or another from the shelves they occupied – could take Lou back instantly to a summer's day in 1938 or a winter's afternoon in 1966 and, once there, allow her to luxuriate in the memories which those notes stirred back to life. The journals contained not simply the facts of the day's events, but the emotions Lou had felt, the thoughts she'd experienced living through those events.

Benjamin pulled one of the journals from a shelf. 1951. He would have been six that year, Lou in her forties.

August 19: beach at Gull Lake. Robert. Sand a washboard beneath our feet. Water warm as a bath. Sun sparkling. Picnic shelter in the trees. Blanket, sun. !!!! Perfect

The journals were Lou's way of ensuring she experienced her life fully, noticing things which surrounded her, the events which enveloped her. It was her way of forcing herself to live intensely.

Lou had begun writing a journal the year she turned six. Each year she bought herself a new journal book: in the early days leather-covered books simply containing lined and dated pages; in later years, books featuring photographs or reproductions of paintings by artists she particularly admired: Monet, Manet, Cezanne, Pissaro. And here it was: an 80-volume record of a life lived. It was like a sprawling novel in 80 chapters. Which Benjamin had mentioned to Lou one time. Some people write their novels, she said. I seem to have lived mine.

Benjamin was reminded of The New Yorker's Joseph Mitchell and his wonderful story of Joe Gould, a man he had met on the streets of New York, a man who carried with him a draft of the great novel he had been writing all his life. And then Joe Gould died. And his great novel died with him. Left behind: a lifetime of scratchings and jottings and scribblings, all of it indecipherable to an outsider.

Benjamin looked at Lou's notebooks, lined up on the shelf near her desk. She was right. These were notes for the novel she never did write, never needed to write. A female Joe Gould. Into two boxes: Save For Benjamin Miles.

Benjamin wondered what kind of novel he was writing with his days. It seemed, sometimes, like a slim volume, all the days passing in a sort of blur. So much observed, so little remembered. He seemed to be skittering along on the surface of life like one of those waterbugs Ethel Wilson wrote about in one of her novels (which one had it been?), the waterbugs contenting themselves with living on the surface of life, only to be terrified now and then when one of their little feet broke the surface and they became aware that beneath them, directly beneath the otherwise benign surface of the water, there were great yawning black depths and who knew what sorts of dangers waiting to consume them... and they skittered away again, sighing a great sigh of relief. That was Benjamin: the skitterer – observations unrecorded, emotions forgotten, not a hint of what he'd done with his precious days.

Indeed, lately he'd been much preoccupied with all that he had failed to do: the books he had not read, the places he had not gone, the fleeting nature of life weighing upon him. He had mentioned as much to Kathleen in one of their after-dinner talks. We don't end up regretting the things we've done, she thought, so much as we wind up regretting the things we haven't done. Human nature, she thought.

The days do run away.

Benjamin circled the room, putting stick-it notes on the things he wanted: some of the framed photos, Lou's record-player, her records, her books.

He slid open the closet doors and pulled from the top shelf a cardboard box marked Snapshot Albums. He pulled it from the shelf and carried it to the bed, sat down and opened it. Wedged between two of the albums, a manilla envelope, folded once lengthwise and inside it, tied with faded blue ribbon, five letters, four of them handwritten.

August 4, 1920

Dear Lou:

I been in the south now for a time, working in an orange grove just outside Tampa. The pay is not much but the work is steady and I am managing to save some little bit each week so my bank acc't is growing.

I have written the boys and heard back from David who is fine and sends his love to us all but no word from Norman so don't know if he rec'd my letter or just does not write back he was never much with a pen was he? It is some time since I heard from him and don't know if he is still at Uncle's farm or has struck out on his own he has always had the wanderlust hasn't he though he is only fourteen yrs old and that is awfully young to be out in the world alone though you know Norman if he gets a thought in his head it would take a team of horses to drag that thought back out and once he decides to do something well that thing will get done. So who is to know.

How are you Lou?

I hope you are managing all right at Uncle Donald's and Aunt Willa's. I know it is hard for you to be there but remember it is only for another short time and then you will be able to be free and on your own and by then I should be a rich man ha ha ha and we can find a home together in N. York.

Don't despair Lou.

One day we will all be together again. In Heaven for certain but I am hoping before that too.

Remember I am always thinking of you every day and keep you in my prayers.

I will write again soon.

Love

Your Brother

Harry

Enclosed is a dollar to buy yourself a treat. Think of me when you are eating that candy Lou. I know how much you love candy.

H.

April 16,1922

Dear Lou

I am sorry to have not written in some time. I have been travelling these past months and am now in Alabama working on a farm. It is hard work – lifting and shoveling and boy am I sore ev'ry night when I roll into bed but I am not staying here much longer for do not like the man who owns this farm he is mean as a chained dog and has a vile mouth and does not always pay us what he owes or when he owes it and so in another week or so whenever I get my next pay packet I will be striking out again, going down the road.

How are you Lou?

I hope you are well and that Aunt and Uncle are treating you with love and kindness, such as you deserve.

Enclosed is a dollar for your next visit to the candy store – do you still like peppermints Lou? Remember that little store we used to go to over on 4th where they had the big jar of peppermints up on the counter? – and pls think of me when you are sitting in the shade of the tree having your treat. I think of you often and mention you and Norman and David in my prayers ev'ry nite. I hope one day soon we can all be together again, though it is a long time I have been hoping for that and asking for it in my prayers and so far my prayers have not been answered

Your Loving Brother

Harry

PS I have not heard from Norman or David in some time though I have been on the move and letters may be going to the last farm I worked on and they would not know where to send them on. When I am situated in a new place and settle in for a period of time I will write them again and hope for a reply.

Have you rec'd a letter from them lately?

H.

June 24, 1923

Dear Lou

I have sad news, Lou. I wrote to Norman at Uncle's farm and rec'd the letter back unopened and with it a letter from Uncle Howard who was saddened to inform that Norman has gone off to California some months since and has been in an accident of some kind and has died of his injuries. Uncle did not say what kind of accident, nor where nor when, except in California someplace. So poor Norman is gone from us and only 17 yrs old. It seems he has lived such a short and a sad life and deserved so much more as he was such a loving son and brother and such a gentle soul though I am sure and certain he has been welcomed into the company of Saints and Angels in Heaven. The only consolation I feel is that he has been reunited with Mother and Father and that one day we will all be able to join them and we will all be together again. I am sorry to have to write you this sad news Lou.

I have written David but have rec'd no letter in reply. I will write Uncle and ask him to forward any news if he has any.

How are you Lou?

I hope you are fine and being cared for well by Aunt and Uncle.

I am working in Georgia these past months. I am working on a peanut farm and the work is hard and the hours are long but the man I am working for is a fine man and a fair man and I am making good wages and am saving as usual so that one day may be we can buy a farm of our own and be together, you and David and me It is my hope anyway.

I enclose a dollar for a treat Lou.

Keep me in your prayers as I always keep you in mine and we shall say an extra prayer ev'ry night for our dear Norman. It is so sad to have lost him. I can still hear his laugh and still see his smile. We shall miss him something awful, won't we Lou?

Your Loving Brother

Harry

October 11, 1923

Dear Lou

I rec'd a letter from Uncle Raymond stating that David no longer resides with them. He left some months ago not saying where he was going and they have not heard from him since and do not expect to so it does not sound as though things ended favourably on the farm, does it?

I fear we may have lost touch with him, Lou, for he does not know where I am living these past months. He knows where you are living and may write to you and if he does pls give him my address and tell him to write to me as well for I am lonesome to think we are being separated in some final way.

I am sorry for David. He is only fifteen yrs and still so innocent and who knows what pitfalls there are in the world for a boy so young and on his own. I wonder what he will do out there in the world at fifteen and what will become of him.

I am still in Georgia and still working on the same farm it is almost a yr now in this one place. Georgia is very hot even in the winter but I am getting use to it and am brown as a berry you might not know me if we passed on the street!

How are you Lou? I hope you are fine. You must be quite the young lady now I bet. Twelve yrs old already. Imagine! Are the boys coming around yet? It is strange for me to imagine you as anything other than that sweet little girl with the beautiful auburn hair. The girl of my dreams.

Write when you are able Lou. Mention me in y'r prayers. And little David too. And Norman, of course.

    Your Brother

        Harry

        (with love, of course)

        Enclosed is a dollar for a treat.

              May 9, 1924

Dear Miss Sutter

I am returning, unopened, the letter you wrote your brother c/o our Farm. Harry left us some months back. He did not tell us where he was headed next. I trust he will write you when he is settled. We miss him dearly. He was a hard worker and a fine young man.

    Sincerely

        Jefferson Handy

        Sumter, Georgia

Wedged between two of the other albums, another manilla envelope marked in Lou's printing: Robert's papers. Inside: Robert's birth certificate, their marriage certificate, Robert's death certificate, snapshots of Robert as a child, snapshots of his parents and relatives – their names penciled on the backs but so faint with the passage of time as to be nearly illegible.

Within the first envelope, a second and within this envelope, two more pieces of paper. The first was a certificate of divorce for Robert's parents. It was dated 1928. The reason for divorce: insanity. The second was a certificate of death for Robert's father. He had died in a home for the incurably insane in the Bronx. Cause of death: Hanging, Self-Inflicted.

William Copeland had been forty-three years of age.

Benjamin read the documents, read them again, folded them and returned them to the envelope.

Between two more albums, another envelope, this one addressed to Lou. In the upper left corner was the return address: The Library, New York Times. Inside, a letter dated the year before last and the photocopy of a news story.

Dear Mrs. Copeland:

Enclosed please find a copy of the story you requested. This is the only story we could find featuring the name Laura Sutter.

The story was dated 12th July, 1918.

> BODY OF WOMAN
> FOUND ON STATEN ISLAND
> The body of 38-year-old Laura Sutter, a widowed mother of four from Brooklyn, was discovered yesterday evening at South Beach. It is believed Mrs. Sutter fell or jumped from the Staten Island ferry. Police said the cause of death was drowning. Foul play has been ruled out.

Beyond the window, the light was failing.

Five twenty-four.

Benjamin put the papers back in their envelope and put the envelopes in the inside pocket of his jacket. He put the box of photographs on the bed: Save For Benjamin Miles.

He took one final look around Lou's apartment, shut the lights, locked the door, left the key at the nurses' station and made his way back through the maze of corridors to the nursing-care wing at the far end of the complex.

Where have you been?

I've been to your apartment.

Oh.

Oh, indeed.

He told her about the need to clear it out, if she wasn't going to be moving back in; the need to dispose of her things, if she was no longer going to need them.

Dorothy told me that you said she could get rid of everything.

Yes.

You don't think you're going to get better, get stronger, get back...

I won't be going back there, Benjamin.

So it's all right if we give your things away? Dorothy said there was a charity that would...

You can take what you want, and give the rest away.

Lou?

Yes?

Perhaps it was the tone of his voice, but Lou opened her eyes, looked directly at him. Yes?

I found an envelope with some of Robert's papers. I hope you don't mind, but I...

Robert's papers?

Some certificates, having to do with his father, his mother and his father.

Oh, said Lou. Yes, she said.

And I found something else, Lou. A letter you received from the New York Times.

The Times?

A letter, and a photocopy of a story.

Oh, said Lou.

The story about your mother.

Yes, said Lou.

You always said she'd died of a broken heart. Now I see what you were talking about.

I always suspected, said Lou. I just never wanted to know. Not in those early years, anyway.

Why not?

The answer would have been worse than the doubt.

And so she had written her own ending to that story. Better a broken heart than a woman climbing up and over the railing of a ferry boat, throwing herself into the night-time waters of Upper Bay; a woman floundering in the sewage-choked waters flushing out to sea; floundering and then allowing herself to become still, willing herself to become still, willing herself to slip beneath the surface, willing herself to sink down to where the chilled waters of the Hudson ran under the waters of Upper Bay, chilled waters which would tug her down and then pull her into Lower Bay where, struggling no longer, she would rise to the surface and float ashore to be found half-submerged in the wave-lapped sand by a stroller, walking his dog at sunrise.

But fantasy, ultimately, is no match for doubt. And so Lou had written to The Times and The Times librarian had been kind enough to do a search of their files and then forward the photocopy. And thus one question had been answered and just one remained. Not the one Benjamin might have thought.

Oh, said Lou. I know why she killed herself. Who could blame her? Four little children to care for, living in a rented flat from which she'd soon be evicted. No money in the bank. No skills, except the skills of a pair of hard-working hands. The man she'd loved down in an early grave. I know why. That's not the question.

Lou looked at Benjamin, then shut her eyes.

The question is, she said, almost a whisper, how could she have done that. Lou opened her eyes. How could she have left us alone like that, the four of us?

Lou shut her eyes and it seemed she was about to drift off once again. Then she opened her eyes: Benjamin?

Yes.

I'm going to ask you something, but before I do, I want you to promise me you'll say yes.

What kind of a...

Promise.

How can I promise...

Promise. Promise me you'll say yes.

Lou.

Promise.

All right. I promise.

I'm very happy you came to see me, Benjamin. I can't tell you how good it's been to have you here. But now I'm going to ask that you go.

Go?

Go home. Go home to Kathleen and the children. Go back to your life. Get on with living. Leave the dying to me.

Lou...

I'm ready to go, Benjamin. I have no concerns about that. And I don't want you to have any concerns, either. You or Kathleen.

Do you remember that line by Swinburne? she said. How did it go?

> Ah, take the season and have done
> Love well the hour and let it go

That's what I'm doing, Benjamin. Letting go. And that's what I want you to do, too. Just let go. Let me go.

Now, I want you to kiss me and say goodnight.

Benjamin did as he was bid.

And when you get home, kiss Kathleen and the children for me. Tell them I love them. Tell them goodbye.

He said he would.

You're awfully lucky, Benjamin. You're awfully lucky to have found Kathleen.

Yes, said Benjamin. I know.

Just as I was lucky to find Robert.

Yes, he said.

Some people go through their entire lives without ever meeting the right person. Or worse, they go through their entire lives with the wrong person.

It was meant to be, said Lou. Just when we both needed someone to come into our lives after losing all those people who had meant so much. And then, when I lost Robert, there were – you and Kathleen and the children. It's surprising the way things work out.

We've been lucky, said Benjamin.

Yes, said Lou. We found someone to love and to love us. That's all you need.

That's a song, Lou.

A song and several thousand poems. And it's true. If you've got love, nothing else matters. If you don't, nothing else will matter. Lou reached out her hand. Benjamin held it in both of his. Lou pulled him closer. Give me a kiss. Benjamin kissed her lips.

Now say goodbye.

Goodbye, Lou. I...

Goodbye Benjamin. I love you. Lou pulled her hand free and turned her back to him and drew her knees toward her chest. Shut the light, will you?

He did. Stood for a moment in the doorway, looking at her. Then turned and went down the corridor, punched the code, walked down the stairs and into the lobby. There was a payphone just inside the door.

Hello?

Hi. It's me. I'm coming home.

Home?

I'll try to catch a flight tonight, if I can. If not tonight, first thing tomorrow morning. I'll let you know as soon as I get something arranged.

Ben?

She's still alive. But she won't be for long. She asked me to say goodbye, and to go home. She wants to be alone.

Silence, seven hundred miles up the line. Then: Ben? Are you okay?

Yes, he said. I'm fine.

Another long silence. Then: I can't talk right now. She was crying. Call me later, okay?

Yes, he said. I will.

Another long silence, then she hung up the receiver.

Benjamin pushed open the front door and went outside, crossed the road and turned around and looked up at the seniors' complex from the far side of the street, looked at the second floor, guessing which room might be Lou's.

Where are you now, Lou?

Lou was dreaming.

In her dream, they were all gathered in the stone-walled, sleepy-treed greenery of a place that looked like Ephrata: were all of an age they had been when they had moved to that little Pennsylvania town in fear and in hope. They were all busy – talking or playing a game (they were some distance off when Lou first saw them) – when David noticed her and alerted the others and then they all turned their smiles upon her and she could hear their voices, a choir of voices, calling her to join them.

Where have you been Lou? We've been worried sick. We've been looking for you everywhere.

We thought you were playing hide and go seek, said Norman.

Hiding behind the markers, said Harry.

And it was then Lou realized they were all within the low stone walls of God's Acre.

And Harry turned his smiling eyes upon her: I told you, he said.

Told her?

That we'd all be together.

We were wondering if you'd ever get here, said Father.

We were getting worried, said Mother.

They were radiant, all of them.

The country air had done them a world of good.

The doctors said it would, said Father. He took Lou in his arms. She could feel the beating of his heart.

In the distance, the Solitary Brethren were at work in the fields, some of them hoeing, some of them ploughing with teams of horses. White-clad Solitary Virgins, hands clasped in front of themselves, were walking in single file from one grey-board building to another, apparently for prayers. From within one of these buildings, the sound of women singing, unaccompanied, their voices thin and pure.

Lou couldn't believe her luck.

Finding them, and finding them all together, after all these years. After all these years of fearing them lost. Imagine her luck.

I told you, said Harry, who wrapped her in his arms. And I always keep my promises.

Where have you been, Lou?

Mother sat down and patted the ground beside herself, motioning for Lou to sit down on the grass beside her. And then they all sat in a circle and waited for Lou to speak.

Well?

Well, said Father, tell us where you've been, since last we were all together.

And Lou began.

She began at the beginning, that day when she had set out, like one of the Solitary Brethren, on her journey into the world.